FIVE CLUES TO A KILLER

A CROSSWORD PUZZLE COZY MYSTERY

LOUISE FOSTER

Five Clues to a Killer; A Crossword Puzzle Cozy Mystery

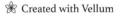 Created with Vellum

This book is dedicated to everyone with a dream.
Dream your dream.
Sing your song.
Make your plans.
Step by step.
You can achieve it.

I'M TRACY BELDEN

And I'm marrying my best friend!

The sun is shining. The birds are singing. No cases on my plate, not a single body in sight, and I have five days off for a honeymoon in Tahoe. Life couldn't be better.

Until my son finds the best man's army buddy floating in a pond. Now, the honeymoon is off.

And the hunt to find the killer and solve the puzzle is on.

1

2 Across; 9 Letters;
Clue: Attendance without being asked
Answer: Uninvited

The forecast for my wedding was clear, with no crime on the horizon.

Though my PI job has interfered with my plans more than once, today had arrived with no cases and, even better, no dead bodies. With _my_ luck there was no telling how the day would end, but for now, life was good.

Langsdale, Nevada, a resort town three hours north of Las Vegas, brings in a lot of cash from rich tourists. Money, passion, and greed add up to violence and felonies. Fortunately, in early April the city has half the heat of summer and half the tourists, which means less crime.

As a faint breeze rolled in off the desert and cooled my cheeks, I breathed a sigh of relief.

Tracy Rae Belden. Five-nine. Thirty-six. Short, brown

hair. Gray eyes. Able to disappear in a crowd without trying. Moderately slim. Okay, I used to be slender. You know what? Let's move on to my husband-to-be.

Kevin Lee Tanner. Six-foot-two. Twenty-eight. Curly black hair. Sapphire eyes. Born with the build and looks of a Greek god. Charming. Loving. Perfect.

Just the thought of him made me smile. Is it any wonder I denied my feeling for him? How could I believe what I felt for Kevin and what he felt for me was real?

No more. After ten years as besties, today was the day.

Outside the small tent set up as my dressing room, lay the Bianco Botanical Garden along with assorted friends and relatives. All of us were waiting for the big moment, which would happen as soon as the minister arrived.

"Are you ready yet?" A flap of the tent let in a world full of attitude in the shape of Marcus, my twelve-year-old Korean foster son. His straight, black hair seemed to reflect the sun even inside the tent. He looked me up and down with a critical eye. "What took so long? You look like you always do."

I gave him a flat look. "Thanks for the compliment."

"No, you look okay." He checked me over again. "Pretty good. I mean *really* good. I guess."

So much for the designer dress I'd borrowed from a client. "Please, stop. You'll give me a swelled head."

Marcus smiled at me. "Kevin's going to marry you no matter what you wear. We're buds. He won't leave me."

"Yeah, that was my big worry, too." I studied my son's smug expression with an upwelling of affection. "This day is all about you."

The boy plopped down on a wicker chair. "Took you long enough to marry him. Now, he gets to live with me all the time."

Can we say self-centered? That was only one of the joys I'd signed on for when I'd taken Marcus, a former street urchin, into my home and heart three years ago. I'd never regretted my decision for a minute.

I couldn't stop a smile. Today everything held a glow. "Is everyone seated? We can begin anytime."

Marcus grimaced. "The minister isn't here yet. When did he call you?"

"Twenty minutes ago. He was half a mile from the main gate." The front entrance is an eight-minute walk from the Japanese section where the wedding pavilion had been set up. I gestured in what I thought was the correct direction, but it was a wild guess. "He should have been here by now."

"You got lost." Marcus never let anything slide.

"I was distracted with thoughts of the wedding." I refused to admit to my well-known challenge when it came to directions. "Besides, there are a lot of paths in this place."

"Sure, there are." Marcus's solemn agreement bordered on patronizing.

Was it petty of me to be comforted that the minister might be as bad with directions as me?

"If he's not lost, he could be dead." A hopeful ember gleamed in my son's black eyes. "He blabbed about a confession and someone killed him."

"Interesting scenario, except we're not Catholic and he's not a priest." The boy's melodramatic theory was a side-effect of his fascination, really an obsession, with my cases. "There will be no murder on my wedding day. Nor at my wedding."

"There's always hope."

I wanted to find the minister and get married without any further talk of crime. I couldn't stand around waiting.

Time to take control. "It's twenty minutes until the cere-mony is due to begin. Let's go find him."

Marcus jumped to his feet. "Kevin said he'd walk to the entrance to look. Rabi must be searching, too. He disap-peared. Bet we find the guy first."

I grabbed ahold of my son's arm as he headed for the front tent flap. "Too many people that way. I don't want to talk to everyone. Let's slip out the back."

I'd tied up one of the rear flaps to let the breeze in. We crept behind a row of hedges without the guests noticing.

The stubble of brown grass had yet to recover from a long winter and a late spring. Manicured designs of pebbles wound past the Japanese statues and shrines. Colorful flags marked the route.

At the moment, the usually calming aura slid right off my growing frustration.

"The main entrance is that way." Marcus pointed to the left. "Kevin went to the English Garden. I saw Rabi walk toward the Japanese shrine."

"Let's check this path." I started walking as I spoke. "It leads to the outcrop that overlooks this whole section."

I was semi-confident about where I was going. Kevin, Marcus, and I were regular attendees on the garden's free days.

Marcus turned around and looked the way we'd come. After a few seconds, he resumed walking. He must have seen my puzzled expression. "I read in a western that when cowboys left their camp, they studied the area so they could recognize it when they walked toward it. You should do that."

"Good advice." After three years together, the boy still underestimates my total lack of directional capability. I've tried every trick in the book. My best hope of returning to my own wedding in time was Marcus.

The rising slope of the ground obscured the rock garden and pond that lay in this direction. With each step, the raised voices of two men became increasingly clear.

Marcus's body stiffened. "That's Rabi."

I recognized Rabi's voice at the same instant. His stern tone of command contrasted with an angry warble from a second man. "Rabi can handle himself."

Jack Rabi, mid-fifties, used to pick up packages for my now defunct full-time job. A black man with skin so dry it looks almost ashen. He has slightly more meat on his tall frame than a cadaver. His shoulder-length black hair falls in perfect waves and glistens as if it's been oiled.

Within a week of moving in with me, Marcus knew Rabi's entire life history, including his twenty-two years with Special Ops.

A second man's strident tone interrupted my thoughts.

Rabi's answer held a sharp edge.

I frowned at the exchange. I couldn't imagine what would provoke Rabi enough to raise his voice.

Rabi not only had more fighting skills than I could comprehend, he was unflappable. When helping on my cases, he'd faced a gunfight, a showdown with a killer, and more than one breaking-and-entering with a slightly raised eyebrow.

Several steps ahead, an ornate metal fence stretched along the top of the rise. The Japanese style wrought iron fence stood almost four feet tall. The open design allowed a complete view of the surrounding area.

I hurried past the row of trees blocking my view. Some people call me nosy. I prefer to think of myself as inquisitive.

In the next breath, I clasped the warm bars of the fence with both hands.

The outcrop rose over the back of the Japanese Shinto shrine where Rabi and another man stood toe-to-toe. Marcus and I were above the men and twenty yards away. Focused on each other, neither one of them noticed us.

They faced each other by a shallow pond, roughly twenty feet wide. Sharp-edged stones of emerald green and deep bronze reflected the climbing sun. The large, rough-hewn blocks, dangerously beautiful, were set along the water's edge.

"Ed." Rabi's commanding tone sounded over the growl of an angry voice. "Emerson, stop!"

The name shocked me. I'd been so focused on Rabi I'd barely looked at his opponent. Now, the other man's familiar face hit home.

Edward Emerson was the leading candidate in the race for the governor's mansion in November. A popular state senator and a decorated veteran from his deployment in Desert Storm, he was favored to win the primary in a few weeks.

Emerson was a barrel-chested man with a solid build reminiscent of a once muscular athlete going to fat. In a swift move that belied his bulk, he feinted to one side then grabbed the slimmer, taller Rabi by the neck, nearly throttling him. "The squad... being killed. Help."

I had to concentrate to understand the guttural words.

Marcus cocked his head to one side. "Choking a guy is a strange way to ask for help."

Rabi swept his arms up and out, breaking the man's hold. He grabbed the shorter man's shoulders. "Calm. Down."

"The guys from Special Ops are dead." Emerson struggled without success to free himself from Rabi's grip. "Supposed accidents."

Three years ago, a guy from the local VFW organized regular poker games for veterans of Special Ops in Nevada. For about a year, Rabi and a few others, including some out-of-towners, got together every few months. Though their ages varied from forty to seventy, their common experiences bound them together.

When the organizer died of cancer last year, the games dropped off. Rabi hadn't gone to one since last spring.

"You. Me." The other man barked out the words in a harsh tone. "Only ones left."

"Make sense." Rabi shook him. "You said a reporter was out to destroy you. You insisted on meeting. Here. Today."

Emerson wrenched himself backward, breaking Rabi's grip. "He knows about the mission. You *told* him. It could only be you. You're jealous of my success. You betrayed me."

"You know better." In the face of the man's growing rage, Rabi remained unmoved. "Tell me about the other guys."

"I tried to contact them. See if you talked to them. If you set me up with the press." Emerson's eyes held a feverish, obsessed look. "Nobody answered. E-mails, calls, texts. Nothing."

"Probably thought you were crazy." Even as I muttered the accusation, Emerson's words struck an odd note. Even in the face of crazy, the other veterans would have given him a hearing.

"Listen to me." The politician raked a hand through his hair. He tried to look in several directions at once. "I think... he may be killing us."

Rabi shook his head. His shoulder length waves glinted in the sun. "Name."

"Jason Olsen, works for some on-line tabloid." Emerson fisted his hands. "We're being picked off."

I gave an unladylike snort. A reporter doing an expose on a mission was tied to several deaths? I tried to track the guy's story, but his wild talk and thoughts of my wedding warred for control of my brain.

Rabi stepped to one side. "A disappearance at sea. A slip off a cliff. A car missing a turn. Accidents."

"Three deaths in three months." The other man's voice skyrocketed toward the hysterical. "That's not a coincidence."

It felt disloyal, but I agreed with Emerson. Crawford, my PI boss, had been on the police force for twenty-five years. First as a uniform cop, then a detective. His never-ending supply of stories has left me wary of coincidences, especially when it involves dead bodies.

"They were trained." Emerson remained undaunted by Rabi's disbelief. "White climbed mountains all over the world. He didn't make mistakes."

Marcus, with his face pressed against the railings, didn't shift one iota. "Actually, that's why they're called accidents. People get careless."

That was the other side of the argument.

As the wind shifted and my designer dress caressed my legs, my own priorities returned full force. Though Emerson's obvious fear aroused my curiosity, I had a wedding to attend, one that couldn't go one without me. My groom was waiting, hopefully with the minister.

I put my hand on my son's shoulder. "We have to get back. Kevin has surely returned by now. He's going to wonder where I am."

Marcus's frowned. "We can't just leave."

"We can't help Emerson." Not that I wasn't curious, but

I'd waited a lifetime to find the man of my dreams. Today was my day.

I told my puzzle-creating brain to stay out of the argument, but the black-and-white grid of a crossword puzzle formed in my mind. Twin lists, Across and Down, were clearly demarcated.

Did I mention that one of my three jobs is creating crossword puzzles? The money barely keeps me in flavored coffee, but it's the one that feeds my soul.

Except I was not going to get involved. I was getting married. In a few hours, I'd be on my honeymoon. Kevin and I would have the weekend to ourselves.

Emerson pounded his fist into his palm. "Someone told. You told. People are dying."

Rabi held up a hand, palm out. "I can't help--"

Emerson's impatient roar echoed off the trees. He bull-rushed Rabi. Head down, the larger, heavier man rammed straight into Rabi's chest.

I heard my son gasp even as I saw Rabi twist his skeletal frame clear of the attack. Quick and tough, Rabi was rarely caught off-guard. Though Emerson caught him a glancing blow, Rabi stayed on his feet.

In a heartbeat, Rabi was behind the other man. Taking advantage of his position, he wrapped one arm around Emerson's neck then locked it in place with a firm grip. A chokehold. Almost impossible to break as long as the grip held.

Rabi's grip would hold until the crack of doom.

Emerson struggled ineffectually until lack of oxygen slowly sapped his strength.

I held my breath as I watched our friend choke the leading candidate for governor of Nevada.

Rabi released his grip and eased his friend to the

ground. He stepped away, waiting until Emerson recovered and cast him a stern look. "Don't think to force me."

The steely tone in Rabi's voice cut through the air.

Marcus shook his head at the warning in our friend's voice. "Rabi doesn't like to be pushed."

No, he does not. I silently agreed. Emerson stood to lose any sympathy he hoped to gain. If the man had been deployed with Rabi, he had to know that tactic would only put his former comrade's back up.

Though my feet and my heart itched to return to the wedding tent, I had to concede that Emerson must be desperate to try to force the issue.

Scared to death one might say.

Crossword clue: What makes a man so desperate?

Answer: A murderer.

2

3 Across; 7 Letters;
Clue: To hunt stealthily
Answer: Stalked

Whether Emerson's story was true or not, the man obviously _believed_ he was marked for death.

I stood on the outcrop, unnoticed by either man. Now I was truly torn. My puzzling brain was fully engaged, but I was about to be late to my own wedding.

From his position on the grass, Emerson looked up to Rabi's six-foot plus height. "I haven't slept. It's been crazy. This reporter's going to destroy me. All for nothing."

"I'll help." Rabi's measured drawl held no animosity. A world-ending tsunami would, no doubt, be met with the same measured calm as flying bullets and deadly threats. "I have a wedding. Best man."

A hint of pride underlay his tone. At least, I wasn't the only one who remembered why we were all here.

Emerson rubbed a hand across his face. Even from this distance, his hysterical edge seemed to have dissipated.

With an outstreched hand, Rabi helped him to his feet. "Come to the wedding. After, we'll talk."

I was so relieved I didn't even wonder how to explain a state senator walking into my wedding. Surrounded by guests which included police officers and PIs, the man would be safe. Kevin would understand. He and Rabi shared the same sense of loyalty to family and friends.

"Come with me." Rabi urged, evidently worried about Emerson remaining alone.

"You've never let me down." Emerson slapped Rabi on the back. While the relief in his tone was clear, the other man's shoulders remained tense. Emerson's scowl returned. "I can't go with you. The reporter is here. I have to stop him."

Marcus's hands tightened on the metal fence. "On your own, you get paranoid. It gets so you don't trust anyone."

The reasoning reminded me of my son's early years, when he'd survived on the street with only his wits.

A fierce protectiveness welled up in me for the young boy who'd entered my life three years ago. I stroked his black hair, warm from the sun. I'd be glad once the adoption process was completed. Then, nothing could separate us.

Emerson's sudden rush into the bamboo caught me by surprise.

"Emerson! Get back here!" Rabi's commanding tone carried over the distance as he strode after his former comrade.

In a heartbeat, like a field of corn swallowing baseball players, the two men vanished into the bamboo stalks.

The puzzle-creating part of me wanted to run after them and get the rest of the story. Was Emerson paranoid? Drunk? Deluded?

Even worse, was he right? Rabi mentioned three accidents. Were they undetected murders?

As the questions multiplied, my feet itched to return to the wedding. I wanted to see Kevin, talk to him. Marry him.

A sudden wind rose out of nowhere, sweeping thick clouds across the sky. Shadows darkened the ground.

The cool April air, whipped into a frenzy, sent cold tendrils snaking under my collar. I glanced at Marcus to reassure him in case the eerie atmosphere bothered him. He stood calm and unmoved.

I glanced up at a blue sky, confused by the soft, white clouds. Had the odd aura been my imagination? I shook off the eerie feeling and squeezed my son's shoulder. "Time to get back. The drama's over."

A frown furrowed Marcus's brow. "It's just beginning. We have to help."

"This is Rabi's business." I added a touch of steel to my tone. "Emerson's worry may prove to be nothing."

"A minute ago, you didn't believe in coincidences." Marcus snorted. "What if the killer finds him?"

I looked at him from my greater height, much as Rabi had looked at Emerson. "The only thing I know is my wedding can't go on without me. No more talk. Move."

Several moments later, I clasped a simple bouquet of peach roses and white lilies while my mother and Mrs. C, my seventy-plus landlady, who was my matron-of-honor, fussed around me.

Rabi had returned without Emerson. For now, the anticipation of my marriage shoved other worries into a closet.

My mother glanced at Kevin standing several feet away. "The groom shouldn't see your gown."

I smiled at her concern for the wedding tradition. However, I was far from a traditional bride. I'd already showed Kevin the dress I'd scored from the client. So, I had no qualms about him seeing me in it now.

Thankfully, Kevin had found our minister hurrying up the path, apologetic about a flat tire making him late. The wedding would be a few minutes late, but I could live with that. Honestly, my only concern was a growing impatience to get on with the ceremony.

I couldn't control what I knew to be a love-sick smile. However, my expression froze when I saw a blond bomb-shell saunter up the path.

Her deep purple dress, gathered at the waist, set off her cascade of golden curls. A matching, wide-brimmed hat, complete with feathers and a ribbon, brought to mind the Kentucky Derby. Even from this distance, I could see her chocolate orbs peruse me with a critical eye.

As I steeled myself for battle with Safina Drummond, my fiancée's twin sister, my gaze slid to the man at her side.

His lop-sided grin was a perfect accompaniment to his leisurely stride. His walking stick and hat would have been in good company at Britain's Ascot Racecourse rather than a former Nevada mining town turned resort.

When he winked and gave me a cheeky nod, I couldn't help but smile. This could only be Fedor, Kevin's cousin. His name had come up during a murder case in November when Kevin and I had unknowingly stepped into the middle of a con game turned murder.

Have I mentioned that Kevin's estranged relatives are a world class band of grifters? Or that he left them when he was eighteen and they framed him for murder? Long story.

Suffice it to say that was when he entered my life, and here we are, at our wedding day.

As much as I adore Kevin, my best friend and the love of my life, I have little use for Safina, and she has less affection for me. She blames me for stealing her brother and life-long grifter buddy away from the family business and her.

"Safina. Fedor." Kevin walked them with a wide smile and open arms. "I wasn't sure you'd make it. Once we decided to take the plunge, our short timeline didn't leave anyone a lot of time to plan."

Safina's manner melted from challenge to affection as she opened her arms and hugged her brother.

It was so like my white knight to cover my back. My heart went into a double rhythm at his rescue.

Kevin glanced my way with a conspiratorial air.

Okay, so maybe the late wedding notification had been part of a master plan. Perhaps I didn't want to feed and entertain dozens of international grifters from his family or an equal number of Kentucky ranchers from my side.

Don't look at me like that. You've never met either set of relatives. Besides, Kevin's twenty-eight. I'm thirty-five and divorced. Neither of us wanted a big wedding. Not to mention, my three jobs barely keep my toe in the lower middle class. Kevin's more stable, but I wasn't going to start our relationship in debt.

My mother touched my arm. "That is the one thing I regret, dear. Your brothers and sister simply couldn't get away from their jobs and the ranch with such short notice. Your cousins, aunts and uncles would also have loved to come."

"I know." At least I sounded disappointed, and I did miss my siblings. I also knew part of the enthusiasm for attending my wedding was Langsdale's proximity to Las Vegas. If my relatives had come, a number of them wouldn't have made it past Sin City. "Kevin, Marcus, and I are planning to come back to visit this summer."

My mother's face creased in a smile. "Your sister can help arrange the festivities. She loves to plan parties."

And attend them. Relieved at having that topic out of the way, I pasted a smile on my face. "I should greet Kevin's relatives."

Who also hadn't received much notice. Who knew they'd show? I glanced behind Safina and Fedor. Any more Feilens? Hopefully, Grandma was too busy fleecing some naïve fool on the French Riviera to make an appearance.

Safina's welcoming smile was all it should be. However, her knowing gaze dissected my cream, mid-calf dress with a discerning eye.

The elegant creation was a Gucci. A loan from a grateful client.

I was in high fashion for the only time in my life.

"Last year's. How appropriate." Safina's smile was sharp enough to cut the wedding cake. "Off white is best, given your age and experience."

I held onto my patience with all ten fingernails. "I've been married before."

The other woman gave me a knowing look. "I'm certain that's not the only misbegotten liaison in your past."

"Okay, ladies, there'll be time for sparring later." Kevin put one hand around my waist and gestured to Fedor with the other. "Tracy, I'd like you to meet my cousin, Fedor Feilen. His list of accomplishments is far too long to list."

The man gave me a roguish wink. "You are ravishing. If you weren't marrying my cousin, I would sweep you away and show you the world."

He was five-ten, slim, with brown, curly hair. He had a

bent nose, but what drew my attention was his rakish smile and intense gaze, shining like a bright flame. His charm had doubtless drawn countless souls into any number of scams.

I could see why he was successful. I put out my hand. "I believe our paths crossed a few months ago."

During the murder case in Vegas when we'd all been after the same Mayan codex.

Fedor drew my hand to his lips and brushed my knuckles with a lingering kiss. "You bested me. That doesn't often happen."

He stole a sideways glance at Kevin before stepping so close that the woodsy scent of his cologne teased my nostrils. "If you come with me, we could paint the world as we wanted it to be."

I couldn't help but laugh as I felt the pull of his promise. "Kevin and I are already painting the world. We have our own business, haven't you heard?"

Surprise lit Fedor's eyes. Then he chuckled.

"I'm sorry I didn't meet you first. I do love witty, intelligent women." Fedor put his hand over his heart and gave an exaggerated sigh. Then, he cast a teasing look at Safina, who'd watched the scene with a knowing smile. "That's why this beautiful lady and I get on so well."

He drew his cousin's hand around his elbow.

Kevin moved closer to my side. "It's great to see you both. Have a seat. We'll begin soon."

His words unleashed a flurry of butterflies and bubbles in my stomach. I waited for Safina and Fedor to move away before leaning against him.

"I never thought I'd see this day." A happy sigh escaped my lips. "Marcus's adoption is on the fast track. We're getting married. Life is good."

Kevin's blue eyes sparkled with affection. Putting his

arms around me, he leaned in, and I raised my face for a kiss.

"Stop it, you two." Marcus's stage whisper broke through the romantic moment. "That stuff's not legal yet."

Kevin shot me a wink before turning to the boy. "Tell me when it's legal. I don't want to miss a minute."

"Oh, ducks, this will never do." Mrs. C waded in with hands flapping. "You shouldn't even be seeing her before the wedding. Certainly, no kissing."

Marcus fisted his hands on his hips. "I told them."

Mrs. C inserted her five-foot-six-inch frame between Kevin and me with determined force. "Kevin. Rabi. Front and center. The minister is in place. Hop to it. Both of you."

I hid a smile as the two men obediently retreated to their assigned positions. I searched for Emerson again, hoping I'd missed him. No such luck. Before I had time to worry, Mrs. C put her hand on my arm and turned me around. I found myself marched to the back of the tent where Mom and Pop waited.

Mrs. C took up a small bouquet and patted her hair in place. "I haven't been a maid-of-honor in decades. Of course, I haven't been a maid--"

"No need to go there," I cut the woman off. "This is a G-rated wedding. Let's get started."

Honestly, the rest passed in a haze of joy. The sun shone. Leaves rustled in the breeze. Birds sang.

Real birds, not like in an animated movie, I wasn't that far gone. When Kevin and I said our vows and exchanged rings, my heart felt like it would zip out of my chest. My blood raced through my veins as if it were filled with sparkling bubbles.

I was no longer alone in the world. He was mine. Together forever.

When the minister finally pronounced us husband and wife, our gazes met in silent accord. We turned as one to face Marcus sitting in the front row. He looked as proud as if he was the matchmaker of the affair, which in a way, he had been.

"Now?" Kevin and I asked as one.

Marcus gave a solemn nod. "Now, It's legal. You can kiss."

And we did. It was glorious.

There was a burst of music. Birds sang.

This time it might have been the animated movie kind.

It was official. Tracy Rae Belden and Kevin Lee Tanner were married. I'd even managed to get four days off from all three of my jobs. That hadn't happened in over ten years.

My PI job had given me the most worry. Crawford, a longtime friend and my boss in the PI biz, was shorthanded due to an appendectomy and a round of flu. One thing I've learned is that crime and adultery stop for no one. But for the last few days no big cases had landed on Crawford's door.

When I'd teased the boss man about his lack of clients, he'd threatened to dig up a murder case for me. As if I'd delay my honeymoon for just any old dead body.

During a lull in the reception line, I leaned against Kevin and gave a long heartfelt sigh. "It seems I've waited all my life for this moment. I'm so glad I married you."

Kevin pulled me closer and softly kissed my lips. "It's you, me, and Marcus now. A family, at last."

My heart thrilled at the protective certainty that rang in his tone.

Since the Feilens crossed him off their Christmas list years ago, Marcus and I, with Rabi and Mrs. C, were the only family Kevin could claim. At least his sister and cousin had come for the wedding. To see Kevin happy, I'd hold in my barbs all day.

Marcus strolled over to us. Munching on a piece of bacon, he broke into our conversation. "When I told my teacher you were getting married on a Friday morning, she didn't believe me. She said nobody gets married before noon on a weekday."

To be fair, my son's teacher has learned to double-check Marcus's stories. "A breakfast brunch is cheaper than lunch or dinner. I got a good price because I chose a weekday. They also threw in the set-up and the teardown at no charge."

"Keeping your eyes on the bottom line is so you, Belden." Kevin gave me a hug. "That explanation makes me grateful I'm not getting married on a cliff at midnight."

My mother strolled up. "The grounds are beautiful. The pond mirroring the trees and the mountains looks like a postcard."

"Kevin, Marcus, and I come here frequently." Another reason I chose the gardens. "Everything fell in place perfectly today."

Except for Emerson and his talk of murders.

The words sounded so forceful I almost looked around to see who said them. Then, I realized my brain was stuck on Emerson's problem. As if the thought had called up a dark aura, a shiver crept up my spine on spider legs.

Though I told myself the man was paranoid, my gut stood firm. Emerson was scared. Was he right? Had the accidents he'd spoken of been murders? If so, had his presence brought a killer to my wedding?

3

---

9 Down; 4 Letters;
Clue: A form of play or sport
Answer: Game

The first, soft strains of music distracted me from my worry. I deliberately focused on my friends and family. It was my wedding day. The realization brought back my grin. I held on to my husband's arm, my husband of less than an hour, and all other thoughts vanished.

Kevin and I made the rounds and spoke with everyone. I couldn't stop smiling though my cheeks ached. Finally, the reception wound down. I put my arm around Kevin's waist. My anchor. My love. My husband. I kept saying that word. I wondered if I'd ever stop.

Mom touched my arm. "It was lovely, honey. I'm so happy for both of you."

"Thanks, Mom." I gave her a hug, kissing her cheek. "You and Pop were great. I'm so glad you're here."

Kevin shook my dad's hand. After I hugged Pop, my parents returned to the table they shared with Fedor and Safina.

A long, slow sigh escaped my lips. The planning. The waiting. The wedding. It was over. I could go on my honeymoon, then get back to my normal life. "It's done."

He put his hand over mine and kissed my cheek. "Mrs. Tracy Belden, my wife."

Cousin Fedor sauntered over on his way to his table, interrupting the moment. His laughing eyes drew my gaze. He kissed my fingers before turning to Kevin with an accusing glare. "Really, Cuz? Lemonade, orange juice, or coffee? You could at least pop for mimosas."

"Not on our budget," I muttered.

Fedor turned his wicked look on me. "Your parents are well-schooled in horse breeding. They have an impressive knowledge of the different breeding for speed tracks in the States versus the steeple chases common in Britain."

"Horse breeding is their life." I hadn't foreseen that a love of horses would be a common interest of our diverse families. "Kevin mentioned you and Safina attend horse races all over the world. I'm glad you're getting along."

"Tracy, now that you're family..." Fedor put a hand on my arm. His fingers danced over my skin toward my wrist in a playful motion. "I have hopes of coaxing you to bring my cousin back to his senses and rejoin the family business."

I laughed out loud. "That is so not going to happen. And if you mention that in the hearing of my son, I'll make you disappear. Permanently."

I raised my glass of lemonade in salute as Fedor's eyes

went wide, then narrowed, all in the space of a flutter of wings.

The other man eyed Kevin from beneath the brim of his hat. "I believe she's serious."

"She is." I chimed in, unwilling to be discussed in the third person.

Kevin shot his cousin a wink. "I'll help cover her tracks."

Fedor threw back his head and laughed. "I can't wait for you and Grandmother to meet."

"Is she in Europe?" Marcus joined us with no warning, approaching at top speed as usual. "When do we leave? Kevin's family would love me."

Fedor tossed me a sideways glance, filled with amusement. "Oh, they would, most definitely."

I sipped my lemonade. "Remember my promise."

"It might be worth the risk." Fedor sauntered away.

When the scam artist stopped to speak with Rickson, a retired homicide detective turned PI, I couldn't help but wonder what those two would discuss. Not horse races.

My stomach growled, reminding me how long since I'd eaten. The guests had hit the buffet after the ceremony. The only food I'd scored were a few veggies and dip while Kevin and I made the rounds.

"Where did you disappear to?" Kevin asked Marcus as the boy scanned the tent, evidently looking for trouble.

Distracted at the sight of Safina flirting with Crawford as their paths crossed, I only half-listened. That boy was always running somewhere, Kevin knew that.

"Too much mush. I needed breathing space." Then, Marcus aimed a narrowed gaze my way. An accusation lurked in the depths of his dark eyes. "I went outside to reconnoiter."

My boss tossed off a wink and a smile at Kevin's sister before he continued in my direction.

Marcus waited until he had my attention. "There's a mannequin in the pond. Did you plan a murder mystery?"

Crawford joined us, groaning aloud. His chiseled features and craggy looks were set into permanent hard edges from his years on the police force. "You did not."

"Of course, I didn't plan a mystery game." My growling stomach distracted me from Marcus's wild talk. "Go eat cake or mints."

Kevin, more on point than I was, tensed.

"Is the next clue on the buffet table?" Marcus asked. "Is Emerson in on the game?"

Emerson's panicky talk of murder returned with a vengeance. My entire body seized. Heart. Lungs. Mind. Everything froze. "What?"

I barely had enough breath to say the word. I wasn't sure anyone heard me.

Marcus did. He rattled out an answer. "The dummy is dressed like Emerson."

That's when the rest of the world stopped. The guests. The tent. The waitstaff. Usually so much quicker off the mark than me, the reality hit Marcus at the same moment.

His eyes widened in horror. "It's not a game."

I felt the blood drain from my face.

My gaze sought out Rabi.

As if the lean man knew my thoughts, he turned toward me and Marcus. He was standing not six feet away. I didn't think he'd heard us, but the stricken look on his face told me differently.

Deep lines etched themselves on either side of his mouth. His eyes, usually unreadable, looked to be drowning in a bottomless abyss.

My heart twisted in sympathy. Emerson had been in fear of his life and I'd been too busy to listen. We... I...

I should have done more. I should have done *something*.

Rabi didn't move for a long, frozen heartbeat. That was an illusion fueled by shock. In reality, when I blinked, the tall, silent man was standing between my son and Crawford.

"Marcus." Despite the circumstances, Rabi's voice came out in the measured tone he always used with the boy. "Show me."

"Call 9-1-1." Crawford, tense as the scene unfolded, pointed at Kevin, not me.

My bossman moved quickly for someone of his bulk. Pushing six feet tall, he was a brick wall of a man. He was halfway across the tent before his words registered.

He scanned the guests as he moved, no doubt cataloguing each person present and their reaction.

Most of the guests consisted of former police, current police, PIs, and a few who walked on both sides of the law. From their furrowed brows and measured looks, a few evidently realized something was afoot. Even my parents's gaze followed Rabi and Marcus as they headed out of the tent.

Crawford, keeping them in sight, snapped his fingers at the huge hulk of a man who'd gone on high alert at the first wisp of tension. "Rickson, nobody leaves."

Rickson rose to his feet, all six-foot-eight of him with shoulders and bulk to match. "We'll wait here."

When he smiled, the ragged scar running down the right side of his face made him more, not less threatening. Knowing Rickson, I had no doubt he was trying to calm the crowd and I'm certain he was sincere. Unfortunately, the entire tent was on high alert.

"Time to mingle," Kevin whispered. Then, he took my

hand in his and addressed our guests. "Crawford and Rabi are checking on a situation. There's nothing we can do right now. Eat. Relax. Enjoy the food and the music."

Then, settle in for the long haul. I had too much experience with finding dead bodies to believe this episode and the subsequent police involvement would be over quickly. Cops are picky when people find corpses.

I hid my worry behind a neutral mask. I couldn't help but feel responsible for Emerson's death. Even as Kevin and I approached the table where my parents sat with Safina and Fedor, part of my brain was tabulating what I'd overheard.

The other part of my brain was watching my honeymoon fade like a mirage in the desert. Rabi would want answers. How could Kevin and I leave now?

Fedor toasted us with a silver flask he'd just drawn out of his jacket. "I hope you don't mind."

I waved him on as he poured a libation in his orange juice. "I have no objection to anyone bringing their own beverage."

Safina gave me a smile under lashes. "A dead body at your wedding. That seems appropriate given your background."

I opened my mouth to begin the sparring match, but my mother spoke first.

She dabbed her mouth with her napkin. "You do seem to be in the vicinity of more than the average number of bodies, dear. I wonder who the poor man is."

Unfazed, Pop gave me a wink. "Another case to share with the guys at the café when we get home."

"She's a body magnet." Marcus rushed up, breathless, with a slight sheen of sweat on his upper lip. Impatient and unwilling to miss anything, the boy would have loved to be in two places at once. "Rabi and Crawford are securing the scene."

The entire tent went silent to hear his report.

Marcus, fully aware of the attention, straightened his shoulders. He paused for a heartbeat to get the full effect. "I'm supposed to lead the police to the pond. They sent one of the wait staff back to inform the administration of what happened and tell them to close the gates."

The crossword puzzle template bloomed fully formed in my mind. Questions zinged through my brain as possible entries in the list of clues.

"Then, get to the front gate." Kevin's comment to Marcus snapped me back to the matter at hand. "Josh, go with him."

One of the younger PIs on Crawford's team began moving as soon as he heard the summons. Stepping in time with my son, he nodded to Kevin as the two exited the tent.

Fedor and I exchanged an amused look. We both knew Kevin's air of command could move mountains. During his years with the Felien clan, my husband's charisma and forceful personality had woven illusions that had parted many a mark from their money.

Fedor's gaze held a look of nostalgia for the old days or perhaps wistfulness for what might have been. For a fleeting moment, sympathy welled up for Kevin's cousin and sister.

The man at my side was a rock of intelligence, loyalty, and wit, plus a thousand other things that made me love him. I stole a look at his profile. Despite what was happening, my heart squeezed in my chest thinking how lucky I was to have him. While his sister and cousin, his companions through his early years, had been forced to watch him walk out of their lives forever.

He was irreplaceable and he was mine.

I looked toward Fedor only to be met with an expectant gaze.

"Well?" Fedor prompted.

For a moment, I feared I'd spoken my thoughts out loud. Safina's expression remained disdainful, but that was normal. So, that was no help.

Kevin touched my arm. "Fedor is impatient. He likes answers up front."

"You, my fine lady." The gentleman in question pointed a silver swizzle stick at me. First, a flask of alcohol. Now, his own personal swizzle stick. What else did the man have in that jacket? "You seem to have the answers in this affair."

I gave an unladylike snort. "I don't even know the questions."

If I did, perhaps Emerson wouldn't be dead.

As if I could have saved a Special Ops vet from a killer who'd murdered three other veterans. I filed my guilt away as a waste of time.

Mrs. C, who has all the skills of a master thief plus enough contacts to make MI-6 jealous, sauntered up to join us. She was unabashedly waiting for answers, as were my parents.

"You are definitely in the know regarding this mysterious body." Fedor gave me a wink. "You and that whirlwind son of yours. We're family now. You can tell us the details."

I wasn't about to be drawn into discussing the case. "I'll tell the police what little I know before I talk to anyone else."

"Ooohh, that's dirty pool." Disappointment colored his words. The swizzle stick dipped. "What has playing by the rules ever gotten you?"

I had to chuckle at his mournful expression. "We all

walk our own road. I'm sticking to the straight and narrow. You might give it a whirl sometime."

Safina's bright red lips loosed in a bright laugh. "Not in this lifetime."

"Or any other most likely." Mrs. C muttered so softly only I could hear it.

"I think you're wise to wait and speak with the authorities, honey." Mom's support wasn't a surprise since she and Pop had instilled their values in me, but I was glad nonetheless. "Since we'll be here for a bit, I'm going to get more of this delicious fruit."

Pop pushed back his chair. "I'll go with you, dear."

After they walked away, Fedor settled in his chair. "Cuz, I can see where living with your new family would be quite the adventure. You have bodies falling all around you."

Taking a sip of her iced tea, Safina arched a carefully tweezed brow. "Is that what you call this? An adventure?"

With a death at my wedding, her underlying scorn was the least of my worries. I raised my cup of coffee. "Either that or a disaster."

My new husband – I loved saying that – only laughed. "At least, it hasn't been boring."

"Good thing, I have an alibi for the entire morning." Fedor's tone turned serious for once. The mischievous glance he shared with Kevin hinted at past adventures. "I also had no motive for killing the man, whoever he is."

Kevin dipped his head in agreement. Any further reminiscing was forestalled when Mom and Pop returned with plates of fruit and cups of steaming coffee.

Pop was barely settled when he eyed Fedor. "Are you two going to the Derby this year? Sounds like you rarely miss attending."

Fedor shifted his attention to my father. "I'm hoping to make it to Kentucky. I like to hit the Derby and Ascot."

Mom paused in the act of spearing a piece of pineapple. "I've never been to Ascot. I would love to attend."

Safina turned a dazzling smile on my mother. "*You'd* fit right in with the Brits. *You* are a lady."

If I hadn't caught the emphasis in her tone, her slanted glance in my direction made her meaning clear. I refrained from rolling my eyes settling instead for a quiet nod of farewell. Kevin and I took advantage of the moment to move away.

"So, my lovely wife." He lingered over the word, evidently as entranced with our new titles as I was, then, he put his arm around my waist and drew me close. "How about sharing the details of the case?"

I shot him a teasing look. "Since you're my husband, I'll trust you."

As we strolled around the tent, greeting people, I filled him in on what Marcus and I had witnessed. With my hand on his arm, I felt Kevin's muscles tighten with each detail.

Though he masked his expression, his protective instincts would come to the fore. Kevin's gaze met mine. "We have to postpone the honeymoon."

I gave a quick nod, happy with the in-sync benefit of our relationship. No way could we leave while Rabi was in danger. He was family.

Nor had I forgotten Emerson's obsession with an alleged murderer. Now, he had been silenced forever and his hard-won knowledge would have to be uncovered anew.

Finding perfectly symmetrical answers is the draw of a crossword puzzle. Once I complete the black-and-white grid, the world makes sense. If only for a moment.

Without answers, my puzzle would never be completed.

Emerson would never have justice. Nor would the accident victims, if they were murdered. Determination to speak for the dead planted itself in my brain.

Kevin's jaw tightened. "Emerson's death proves his argument. That leaves Rabi as the sole survivor of their poker club."

"Marcus was right." Which the boy would be the first to point out. "We're going to have to find the killer."

4

---

33 Down; 7 Letters;
Clue: Deal with a problem
Answer: Confront

I f you've never been questioned by the police about a violent death, my advice is to avoid it. They get paid to suspect everyone.

Fortunately, most of my guests were milling around the tent all morning. Unfortunately, it's hard to keep track of milling people. After all, Marcus and I snuck away unseen. Kevin and Rabi were also gone for a time.

Not that Marcus or I needed an alibi, but I felt oddly relieved we'd been with each other. Kevin returned with the minister. Rabi, however, left and returned alone. Naturally, he told Crawford then the police of his confrontation with Emerson.

Thankfully, Marcus and I were able to back up Rabi's

version, including his promise to help his former comrade. However, he did chase Emerson into the stand of bamboo.

While the police interviewed everyone, Marcus, Kevin, and I sat patiently at the table.

Well, Kevin was patient.

If you believe I was patient, you don't know me.

If you think Marcus stayed at the table for more than a nano-second at a time, you've learned nothing.

To pass the time, I jotted down what I remembered of Emerson's words to Rabi. "I'll check with Rabi and see what I missed. I couldn't catch every word."

Kevin patted my arm. "I'm sure you tried."

Though his voice oozed sincerity, I didn't have to look at him to know he was laughing at me. "I like to have the story straight."

"The police are a suspicious lot."

This time his tone was definitely patronizing.

Marcus interjected himself between Kevin and me with no warning. "We got problems."

Kevin waved to my mother across the room. His expression friendly. "What did you learn?"

Marcus pitched his voice low. "Five people in two different groups told the cops Rabi attacked Emerson. They heard Emerson say Rabi was out to destroy him."

Breath escaped my lungs at the gut punch.

Kevin took the news with no sign of concern. "We had to expect that."

Tension radiated from my son's thin frame. "All the police needed was an excuse."

Marcus had become friends with several police officers and detectives since meeting Crawford. He knew the men and women were good people, but worry for Rabi had thrown the young boy's brain back to his days on the street.

As a homeless loner, he'd been suspicious of everyone, especially the authorities.

"None of us will let Rabi go down for murder." Kevin put a hand on Marcus's shoulder. My hubby's expression softened into a rueful smile. "Your mother is too obsessed to quit until she completes the puzzle correctly."

The stiffness in Marcus's shoulders melted.

A warm glow flared to a tidal wave of affection. My family. I put my hand over Kevin's tan one on the table. The knots in my gut loosened.

Kevin twined his fingers with mine. "You don't want Rabi to be in trouble. It's clouding your judgement."

I released a long, slow breath. My gut had been tied in knots from the moment I knew Emerson was dead. Rabi was a perfect suspect. The police would be derelict not to look at him as the possible killer.

Despite our wedding day's tragic turn, confidence glittered in Kevin's gaze. "Forget the wedding. It's over. Focus on the puzzle. It's what you do best."

A weight lifted off my shoulders. My mind tracked what little I knew. "Rabi wouldn't hurt Emerson."

"If he did, he wouldn't be so obvious," Marcus whispered.

The boy's cynical attitude caused me to pause in my heartwarming speech but I carried on. "Emerson was looking for a killer. The murderer is still on the loose."

"He could be among us, even now," Marcus spoke in the low voice of a noir movie announcer.

"Are you done with the drama?" I gave my son a mock glare. "This killer is too cautious to be sitting in our tent waiting to be interviewed by the police."

Though Marcus didn't move, energy radiated off of him like an electric current. "We're on the job."

Kevin read my shifting mood. Our long relationship as friends and partners had lain the foundation of deep familiarity. "The Jane Austen Society was in the English Garden."

Another group of needles in a haystack. "The killer could have wandered in with them."

"Or not." An aura of a caged panther surrounded Kevin. "Emerson was too well known to walk through the front gate."

"So, there's a back way in." I seized on the point as I faced my son. His gleaming eyes met mine. "Chat up the staff. Find out what groups are on-site. How many individuals entered. Security cameras. Tapes."

Marcus's eyes narrowed. "I can ask for copies for my school project."

I couldn't believe they'd hand tapes to a child for an imaginary homework assignment. "The police need a court order to get security tapes."

"I'm a little kid scared of a killer." His lip quivered. In the next heartbeat, he dropped the act. "I'll see what I can find out."

"If anyone can do it, Marcus can." Kevin clapped him on the shoulder. "Go get 'em, tiger."

Marcus stepped away, then stopped. "Wouldn't it be cool if the minister did it?"

Before I could respond, he was gone.

Rickson, one of my fellow PIs in Crawford's business, entered the tent, letting in a sliver of sunshine as he swept the flap aside. He strode toward us with a heavy stride. His six-foot-eight-inch frame overshadowed everyone else.

Kevin held his hand out to me, standing in the same instant.

I stood with him, as relieved as him to be on the move.

As Rickson joined us, I tried to contain the questions ready to burst forth. "What's up?"

"CSU is finishing." He studied the people as he spoke. "Detective Wilson is grilling Rabi. They're stopping the media at the gate, but word will leak out. You solve the case yet?"

I chewed my lip. Emerson's death would be high profile. The pressure to solve would be intense. "How could I?"

My tone and words were sharper than I'd intended. I grimaced in apology.

The next thing I knew I was enveloped in a teddy bear hug by a grizzly bear. "It was still a good wedding."

He released me with a whoosh.

Slightly off balance, I found I could breathe again. It took me a moment to gather enough air to restate the question. "What did you see?"

Rickson met my gaze. "Rabi never left the tent once the wedding began. By then, Emerson was dead."

My heart seized. I went on the defensive. "Does Wilson have enough to arrest Rabi?"

Rickson met Crawford when they were partners on the force, first in Vegas, then in Langsdale. "I've booked people on less. He'll be pressured to make an arrest. But the DA's new. He won't want a mistake."

Kevin rubbed my shoulder. "That'll buy Rabi time."

Rickson went into full detective mode. "Emerson confronted Rabi about a betrayal. A killer who murdered three Special Ops vets. Men who trusted Rabi. He could have gotten close enough to kill them. He's trained. He's the last man alive in their circle of friends."

The wheels in my mind started spinning. "Emerson was meeting a reporter, who he believed was out to destroy him."

Kevin stiffened. "You said Emerson was practically unhinged. Olsen and Emerson could have fought."

"The reporter hasn't been found." Rickson tapped me on the shoulder. "Rabi's good people. If you need anything, let me know."

"Thanks." I covered his hand with mine then watched the big guy walk away. He didn't miss much. Unfortunately, he had to leave later today for an out-of-town case. So, he wouldn't be around to help.

Kevin and I had only walked a few feet from our table. There was really nowhere to go. With a silent agreement we strolled back and sat again. I danced my fingers lightly across his hand. "We need information on Emerson. I wonder what Mrs. C could pull out of her hat of contacts."

The caterers had started to clear up. My hopes rose. If the police let them leave, the rest of us should soon follow.

The band, okay it was a DJ, one guy with his own equipment, was packing away his cords with jerky movements. His shoulders were as tight as a stretched rubber band.

The silence finally registered. Though the cops said they didn't care about the music, the guy had stopped playing a while ago.

As I scanned the tent, I met the DJ's glare. What did he want? This wasn't the wedding I'd planned. My gaze was moving on when he threw down a cord and marched toward me.

Within seconds he had both of his long, slender musician hands splayed on top of the table. He leaned down, directly in my face. "I refuse to play under these macabre circumstances."

Did he honestly think I cared? "As soon as the police release you, you can go."

His lips turned up in a sneer. "That's it?"

The harsh, accusing tone jabbed at me like pinpricks.
"I'm not in charge. If you want to go, ask the police."

The thin man looked down his nose at me. He folded his
hands across his chest, drawing attention to his garish red
and green striped shirt. "I insist you pay my fee for the
entire time I am forced to remain on-site."

I stared at him as a bubble built inside of me. Did he
believe he was going to get extra money from me?

Kevin's expression held a measure of sympathy as he
looked at the guy. Despite my hubby's iron-like control, one
corner of his mouth tipped up.

This DJ was getting on my last nerve. I eyed him without
bothering to stand. "You played music for half-an-hour
before the ceremony and maybe fifteen minutes after. You've
been stuffing your face with my food ever since. At this
point, you should be glad you have half your fee. It may be
all you receive."

His gasp held every evidence of true outrage. He threw
back his shoulders. "I have a live performance tonight and
that police interview was very traumatizing. If I can't
perform, I will sue you for mental anguish."

He obviously had no idea who he was dealing with.

I wanted to tell him as much, but I couldn't get the words
out. Giggles, laced with a touch of hysteria, bubbled up and
exploded.

In the face of my laughter, the DJ's mouth flapped open
and shut. "I mean it."

"Seriously?" That was all the farther I got. I was laughing
so hard I couldn't get another word out. Sue me?

For what? The paint supplies Kevin and I had invested
in?

After a moment, he turned to Kevin and opened his
mouth.

My hubby's stern expression stopped him. "We'll cover your fee as agreed. Nothing extra. Leave before she quits laughing or I won't be responsible."

After one look at Kevin's steely eyes and set jaw, the DJ shut his mouth with a snap. He cast me one last fiery glare then stomped away.

After another moment of giggling, I regained control and dabbed at the tears that threatened to ruin my makeup. I leaned against Kevin's shoulder and took a deep breath. "That was worth it, that guy is clueless."

Kevin's shoulder rose and fell under my cheek. "It was worth a shot. We might have paid him off."

The Belden Tanner family is a very non-judgmental group. That's one of the things I love about us. With that tangent, my brain jumped onto a carousel of random thoughts.

Regret that Emerson was dead. A wish Kevin and I had eloped. Jealousy that my husband *was* so sickeningly patient. It was his wedding day and he didn't look the least bit irritated that the police were running a murder investigation.

Yes, I'm a petty person, but someone in this relationship has to be.

Seriously, he simply sat there studying every person in the room, while flipping an 1896 Liberty silver dollar over and under his fingers. Then the silver dollar disappeared. He pulled a deck of cards out of his inner jacket pocket and started shuffling them.

I straightened in my chair. He brought a deck of cards to our wedding? "Were you expecting to be bored? Or do you plan to start a poker game?"

"A game would pay for the honeymoon." He flashed me a swoon worthy smile. "They're my wedding present from you. The ones with a picture of your home ranch on the back."

I'd had them made at the Silver Mining Five and Dime, an over-the-top tourist attraction three miles from my apartment that boasted every keepsake anyone could dream up.

"The entwined B and T on the gate is a nice touch." He showed me the image, then gave me a wink. "How could I leave them behind on my wedding day? They remind me of you. My best friend. My wife. My partner for life."

His voice deepened with each word. He leaned closer and planted a soft, gentle kiss on my lips. "You are a prize I never thought the Fates would grant me."

Could anyone be annoyed at this man? With my toes curling in my shoes and my blood turning to warm honey, I could barely think.

Then, with a serene expression on his too handsome to be true face, he shuffled the cards in one of a hundred fancy ways. Sometimes faster than my eyes could follow.

My tension eased as I watched his practiced hands flow from one trick to the next. He dealt me four queens. I was excited, then amused when he gave himself four aces.

His expression held no regrets. "The house always wins."

A lesson worth remembering. Rabi was alive. Everyone else, including Emerson, was dead. Aces and eights. Deadman's hand.

Marcus sauntered up to the table, sat down, and eyed me with a smug expression. "The gates opened to group activities at nine. Emerson didn't come through the gate."

"A point for Kevin." I noted.

My hubby frowned. "Makes the job harder."

The boy nodded. "Reporter didn't come through the gate either."

"Did anyone pay admittance but me and Kevin for our guests?" This bordered on annoying. "How did Emerson and the reporter get in? Not to mention the killer."

"Your and Kevin's wedding, the Jane Austen wannabes, and a yoga class were the only groups on the grounds." Marcus ignored my outrage. Smart kid. "The yogis were in the main building looking at the greenhouse when security rounded them up for the cops."

Kevin trailed his fingers down my arm, almost short circuiting my brain. "Back roads for deliveries. Special entrances for events. We need to find a map. Emerson attended a fund raiser here last fall."

I did a double take. "He did?"

"His whole staff would know about loopholes in security." Marcus didn't waste time asking about Kevin's knowledge of current affairs. He focused on suspects.

I shifted back to the case, adding a note to get a list of Emerson's office staff. "The reporter could have followed Emerson inside. He heard him argue with Rabi. Confronted him for the truth about the mission."

"What truth?" Kevin asked.

"I have no idea." I admitted. "Emerson didn't go into detail."

Marcus leaned halfway across the table. "Emerson said the truth would ruin him."

I saw a clear path to my honeymoon. "Olsen threatened Emerson. They fought. Emerson was accidentally killed."

Of course, that's not what happened. My life has never been that easy.

5

47 Across; 9 Letters;
Clue: Intended to distract someone's attention
Answer: Diversion

Moments later, Marcus had left to wheedle more information out of the security guards.

I was tempted to stroll down the path and see if anyone would stop an escaping bride. "I'm going to find Wilson and demand an update."

Kevin didn't raise his gaze from the flashing cards in his nimble fingers. "Crawford's back."

I'd seen little of my bossman since he left the tent to check out the dead body. I'd been hoping his contacts on the force would provide a window into the initial findings on Emerson's murder.

Gazing through my lashes, I eyed my boss's heavy tread as he walked across the tent. He nodded in greeting to a group of former polices detectives who, like me, now worked for him. His wide, craggy face was set in a grim expression, but that was normal. He looked no different than he always did, except he didn't so much as glance at me.

What was up? I'd known him longer than I'd known Kevin. My gaze swept over him, taking in every detail.

Crawford's meaty, scarred hand pulled his suit jacket together over his broad chest and buttoned the buttons.

I pointedly returned to watching Kevin deal poker hands in his favor. "Crawford has news, and I'm betting it's not going to help the good guys."

Notching my peripheral vision up to red alert, I watched Crawford proceed out the other side of the tent.

Questions of why, who, and when, set my brain spinning like a tilt-a-whirl. A murder. My wedding. My honeymoon. This was shaping up to be a lost weekend. "I called the rental in Tahoe. They said it would cost twenty-five percent of our payment to cancel now. Our balcony suite is open next weekend. They should let us move it at no cost."

Kevin laughed. "They have my sympathy, but my money's on you for the win."

I was actually looking forward to arguing with them. "I'm not paying for a honeymoon I didn't get, and I'm getting this honeymoon. Mark my words."

"I'm with you, ducks." Mrs. C chose that moment to trundle up to the table. She settled into the chair next to me with a piece of wedding cake surrounded by pastel mints. "My bridge club had great fun making the mints. They're thrilled you're finally taken. They'd all given up hope, don't you know?"

Having snared one of the tasty treats, I paused with it halfway to my mouth. "What is this, the Middle Ages? Women don't need to get married to have a good life."

The older woman frowned. Then, she licked a bit of frosting off her fork. "It's naught to do with you. They're eager to see Kevin now that he'll move in to our building."

"Oh, I get that." I popped the mint in my mouth and let its tangy coolness melt on my tongue. How quickly could I follow Crawford outside? Why didn't he just talk to me?

I caught a sideways glance directed at me from one of the uniform officers at the entrance.

"I didn't mean to offend you." Mrs. C's shrill tone carried in the enclosed space. She put a hand on my arm and leaned in. Her eyes shone with an inner spark. "Do you need to speak with Mr. Crawford? A diversion, eh?"

Ignoring the underlying thrill in her voice, I shook my head. "I'll wait a bit, go out, and find him."

"What's the fun in that?" My son's disappointed sigh sounded at my back. "Besides, it's too obvious."

"Not to mention too easy for you," I shot back.

"The cops are watching." Marcus's voice carried an undertone of doom. "That's why Crawford didn't talk to you. The tent flaps have ears."

He chuckled at his own weird joke.

When my son isn't a junior PI, he's a twelve-year-old boy.

Kevin grinned despite situation. "Go for it, Mrs. Colchester."

"I'll help." My son's whisper didn't carry beyond our immediate circle.

"I'll keep all eyes on me." Mrs. C delicately forked a bite of cake into her mouth. "Give me two minutes."

The whole episode was a bit too James Bond for me, but since there seemed to be no stopping them, I decided to lay down ground rules. "I want my deposit back on this tent and the equipment."

I felt more than saw Marcus melt away.

The older woman set her napkin next to her plate. "I believe I'll stretch me legs."

Patting her white curls in place, she crossed behind me, touching my shoulder in the process.

I didn't follow her progress. I didn't want to know what she was planning. Better deniability. I turned to Kevin, busy gathering his deck of cards. "Why would you give them free rein?"

He tapped the deck into the case, then slipped it into his inner pocket. "Crawford doesn't play games with the police on a homicide. He could have sat with us. He didn't."

A growing sense of trepidation tied my gut in knots.

Kevin's mouth turned up. "A little diversion will help everyone's mood."

"My dear man!" Mrs. C's offended scream almost drowned out Kevin's words.

A squeal of a keyboard and a bellow, I believe from the DJ, followed on the heels of the scream.

Kevin held out his hand to me. "Shall we?"

I let him draw me to my feet. With my dewy-eyed gaze glued on my husband, I walked with him in a casual stroll aimed toward a slit in the side of the tent.

"What are you doing to her? Owww!" Marcus's high-pitched squeal of pain proved to be ear-piercing in the enclosed space.

"That's a bit over the top, don't you think?" I whispered.

Kevin shook his head. "People love drama."

The guests proved him right. Every person in sight turned toward the raucous scene behind us. The tide of guests and staff moved like a single wave, including the uniformed police officers positioned at the entrances.

"Here now!" Fedor added an English accent to the scene. "Watch yourself, my good man. How dare you?"

"Ooooh, you poor thing." Safina's liquid tone managed to be heard over everything else.

"It's a family affair. That's nice." On that happy note, I slipped through the flap. With the sun's warmth on my face and a cool breeze on my skin, a sudden silence fell. For all the noise inside, very little of the hubbub carried beyond the tent.

Kevin touched my arm and nodded toward a row of thick, eight-foot-high ornamental grasses. The closest possible hiding spot for someone of Crawford's size.

As soon as we rounded the thicket of grasses, bossman pointed toward the tent. "There goes your deposit."

"I warned them."

His smirk vanished in a heartbeat. The somber expression that replaced it didn't bode well. "Rabi's gone."

I nearly choked. "Taken for questioning? Arrested?"

Kevin's sapphire gaze studied Crawford with enough heat to burn a hole through steel. "Took off."

Crawford nodded. "The fight before the wedding was witnessed by two other parties besides you and Marcus. So was his late arrival before the ceremony."

"He wasn't late." The disclaimer sounded weak even to my ears.

Rabi hadn't arrived at the wedding area until a few minutes after Marcus and I returned. It wasn't long but obviously the police knew of the timing, and as mentioned, they tend to be suspicious.

I bit my lip, weighed down by worry.

Sympathy glittered in my boss's gaze. "Rabi said he lost Emerson in the bamboo. He didn't want to miss the wedding to continue searching. He saw no one else. Doesn't help his cause."

Kevin's intensity was palpable.

I struggled to absorb his news, realizing we didn't have much time. "Anything else?"

My boss's usual blaring tone was lowered to a gravelly whisper. "Emerson's skull was cracked. Looks like he hit one of the rocks and landed in the water. The ME said she'll know more after the autopsy."

I filed the facts away for later.

"Bruises will develop on his neck where Rabi choked him." My boss continued his report without inflection. "Have to wait and see if any develop on his back."

Kevin's eyes narrowed. He gave my hand a reassuring squeeze.

I'd missed something. My brain whirled, looking for an answer.

"If he was held under." Crawford cocked his head to one side, evidently gauging the noise in the tent. "Don't call him or talk to him on your phones. Get burners. Don't surrender your cell phones if the police ask. They'll be watching you. You're his closest known associates."

I nodded at each admonishment.

"Do not interfere with an active murder investigation." Crawford admonished. "You know the rules."

I gave an unladylike snort. He knew Kevin and I wouldn't play by the rules where family and friends were concerned. "You warned us. You're covered."

"I'll do what I can, but Rabi didn't help himself or me." Crawford's glare could have cracked a diamond open. "I just finished reminding Wilson how he'd look if the arrest fell apart in three days."

I knew I could count on my bossman. "I appreciate it."

"You're nothing but trouble." His wide mouth turned up, before he strode away without another word.

Kevin and I walked to a trail past the ornamental grasses. A moment later, we reversed course and holding hands, approached the tent. We'd barely stepped into the sunlight when a sharp-eyed, harried looking white, male uniformed officer approached us.

"You were told to stay in the tent." His accusing tone put the blame for our escape squarely on our shoulders.

"It's our wedding day." Kevin's tone was neither angry nor defensive. "We stepped outside."

"I never heard anyone say I couldn't leave the tent." It's amazing what you don't hear when you choose not to listen.

The officer's frown deepened. "Detective Wilson wants to speak with you. Now."

Kevin and I obediently walked to Detective Wilson's mock-up interview room, which was the smaller tent I'd dressed in.

Wilson, a lanky white man with straw-like hair and the build of a scarecrow, stared lasers at us.

To save time, I'll skip the back and forth and sum up the interview. Kevin and I couldn't help. Since neither of us had seen Rabi leave, we could also honestly swear we had no idea where Rabi *might* have gone.

It took a bit to convince Wilson, because he knew the lengths I'd go to in order to protect a friend.

"We're done." Without warning, Wilson pointed a long, slim arm at Kevin and me. "If you hear from Rabi, tell him to contact me. I have questions for him."

"Sure thing." I'd tell Rabi anything if I saw the man.

Kevin stood but made no move to leave. "How much longer are you going to detain our guests? Some of them have planes to catch."

"The guests have been told they can leave." Wilson swept his hand through the air. "I have everyone's statement as well as their names and addresses. Get out."

That was a bit rude for a public servant. I took a half a step forward. "Did you get the names of the catering staff and the botanical garden staff that were on the grounds?"

"Of course, I --" He broke off and aimed a frown my way.

I favored him with a smile. "Could I get those names? I'd like to thank them. Send a card perhaps."

Wilson's fisted hands shook slightly. His narrowed gaze bored into mine. "This is an active homicide investigation, Tracy. Do not interfere. Not even for your friend."

I put a hand on my chest in shock. "Absolutely not, but the names..."

"You are not on this case." Wilson clipped off the words. "You are not to investigate. Either of you."

My new hubby nodded agreeably. His expression as sober as a judge.

I could almost believe him. I wonder if Wilson believed me.

The detective took a deep breath. The angry red flush in his face receded. "I know he's your friend, but let me do my job. Stay. Out. Of. My. Case."

He underlined each word with special emphasis. Evidently, he wanted me to know how much he really meant what he said. I put on my innocent mask. "I understand completely."

Kevin studied Wilson for a moment, managing to imbue the air with a sense of comradery. "No one's ever thought to just warn her off. I'm sure that'll work."

As soon as the sarcasm hit him, the tight set to Wilson's shoulders eased. His mouth eased into a rueful smile. Wordlessly, he pointed to the entrance.

Kevin put his hand around my waist and we walked out of the tent. "Thank you for your time, Detective."

Emerson's death. Crawford playing the spy card. Rabi leaving. Wilson's warning. By the time the thoughts raced through my mind, Kevin and I walked into the main tent. In the short time since we'd left, the place had gone from being full of bored guests to empty of all but our families.

Marcus ran up to us, eyes alight. "I knew they wouldn't arrest you. Nothing to hold you on."

I put a hand on his shoulder. Then, pointed to corner where the DJ had been set up. Based on what I'd heard as I was leaving, I could only hope *he* wouldn't take me to court. "No injuries? No damages?"

My son's mouth bowed up into a Cheshire Cat grin. "We're too good."

Fedor sauntered up. "For once, I regret having to return to the Riviera. I sense this is the beginning of another adventure."

Since Kevin and I had intended to leave for our honeymoon this afternoon, his relatives had only flown in for the day. Mom and Pop had plane tickets back to Kentucky on an afternoon flight. Considering the circumstances, I preferred everyone's quick departure.

Safina walked up. Her chocolate brown eyes studied Kevin with a searching intensity. "I hope you're happy."

The words, so often used as a scathing retort toward me, were full of affection.

Kevin's warm gaze, as blue as a cobalt sky, smiled at her. "I am, sis. Thanks for coming."

I watched the twins, resisting the urge to put my hand on his arm. Instead, I looked at Safina. Family comes first where I come from and she was family now. Kevin's and mine. "I'm glad you made it to the wedding. You'll have to visit when you can stay for a few days."

I can play nice when I want to.

The younger woman paused before answering. "Take care of my brother. I want him to be happy. Perhaps you'll surprise me."

Then she congratulated me. Not Kevin, just me.

What a sweetie.

Though her expression held little warmth when she eyed me, her gaze held no animosity. "Take care of him."

"I will," I promised.

Fedor bowed at the waist and shot off a quick wink. "I can't wait to spend more time with your little family. Ahhh, what we could do together. I'll be sure to visit again."

Kevin tapped his chin. "Were you included in Tracy's invitation?"

"Tracy and I are like this." Fedor wound two fingers together. In the face of my raised brow, he tossed me a kiss. "Good luck clearing your friend. Perhaps I should have a word with the authorities about staying out of your way."

The very thought sent a shiver up my spine. "You don't want to miss your plane."

"Good-bye, Fedor." Kevin's voice held a finality. "Keep 'em guessing, Safina."

A warm smile wreathed her face. "Always, bro."

On that note, the twosome pivoted toward the main entrance of the now deserted tent.

Mom and Pop were the only others still remaining. They said farewell to Fedor and Safina, then the pair of grifters walked into the April sunshine and disappeared.

Pop rubbed his hands together as he and Mom closed the distance to us. My father let out a loud bark of laughter.

"That DJ lit out of here like he had a burr under his saddle. No one saw you two leave. Good job, Marcus."

He nudged my son's shoulder, who puffed out his chest at the compliment. "Mrs. C was great, as always."

My mom cast me a worried gaze. "Is Mr. Rabi in trouble? He's such a quiet man. Like the still waters of a pond."

"I couldn't have said it better." Second to horse ranching, my mom was a born people watcher. "We're going to have find out what's going on beneath that surface."

"You'll finish this puzzle. You've never let one beat you yet." Pop's expression lit up as he met my gaze. "Another case for my baby girl. Wait'll I tell 'em back home."

Warmed by his confidence, I took one last look around the tent. The deft hands of the botanical garden crew were busily tearing down the venue. Chairs were stacked neatly on wheeled carts. Tables were being folded up. Next the tent would go. Soon the grass would pop back up as if we had never been here.

"We'll drive you to the airport," Kevin offered. "Thanks to the police interviews, you don't have as much leeway to catch your flight as planned. I'm glad you came in a few days early so we could spend time together."

"It was such a nice visit, up until the murder." Mom put a hand on Kevin's arm. "You'll have to let us know when you're coming to Kentucky, so we can plan a get together for our family and friends at home."

Pop squinted under the bright sun as we stepped out of the tent. "Marcus, keep us posted on what happens."

"You bet." Marcus tossed off a nod before glancing at me. Worry gleamed in his dark eyes.

I pulled him to my side for a quick hug. "Pop's right. The Belden Agency has never let a puzzle beat us."

Though the case percolated in the back of my brain, I

put it aside. I couldn't give Emerson's murder my full attention until Mom and Pop were safely delivered to the airport.

The boy slid a quick look at Kevin. "It's the Belden-Tanner Agency now, isn't it?"

"That's right." Kevin snapped his fingers. "I get equal billing."

I aimed a cool smile at my new partner for life. "Then you'll have to pull your weight in this case."

Not least was finding Rabi before anyone else did, including the police or the killer.

Why had he left? Where had he gone?

And would we find him in time?

6

19 Across; 5 Letters;
Clue: Serious; Somber
Answer: Grave

A short time later I stood outside my loft with Kevin and Marcus. The three of us had walked into the apartment thousands of times in the past three years.

This time was different.

Once Kevin and I started dating, we quickly realized we wanted to spend our lives together. With the wedding so close, we agreed he wouldn't spend the night until it was official.

We wanted to make our marriage a transition to a new life for all three of us. Another reason we'd pushed to be married as soon as possible.

Kevin had moved his possessions into the apartment over the past week; his clothes, artwork. One piece I'd loved for years was a painting of a horse jumping over the moon amidst a field of stars. He didn't have a lot of furniture, but the pieces were definitely better quality than my thrift store buys and Goodwill rescues.

When Kevin took his keyring out of his pocket, Marcus held out a small, flat box. "...got you something."

The boy's tentative tone surprised me.

Kevin pocketed his keys and took the box. After untying the ribbon and opening the lid, he paused.

I've rarely seen Kevin at a loss for words. His entire life consisted of lessons on how to think on his feet.

He stood transfixed, staring at the present. He swallowed hard and pulled out a small gold keyring with a single key on it. The outline of a house held three tiny figures standing side by side.

"It's us." Marcus scuffed the toe of his shoe on the floor. He looked up at Kevin. "A mom and a kid... and a dad. Right?"

Kevin swallowed again. "Absolutely. Belden's your mom and now, I'm your dad. Always."

My eyes blurred with tears. "None of us will ever be alone again. We're family."

The next moment we embraced in a group hug with Marcus in the middle. Of course, the boy child was the first to wiggle free.

Kevin opened the apartment door with his new key, then stepped aside. He looked at Marcus and me with love in his eyes. "Welcome home."

When the door behind us, I felt as if we'd locked the world away. "Home. The three of us."

Marcus grimaced. "Are you going to get mushy?"

"Yes," Kevin pulled me close and kissed me.

As I wrapped my arms around his neck, I thought I

heard Marcus say "Yuck" as he walked away. When we came up for air, I met Kevin's gaze. "I want you to know I slept on the couch last night. It was a great sacrifice with your fancy bed, padded mattress, and silky sheets taunting me."

Kevin kissed me again. "I appreciate your control. Silver lining from today is... we get to sleep in *our* bed tonight."

"And I won't be alone," I whispered. Ever again.

"Come on." Marcus slapped the kitchen table for emphasis. "We have a case. I'm not doing all the work. That's child labor."

I heaved an exaggerated sigh and walked toward the kitchen. "I'm good with you doing the work as long you don't tell your social worker. Now that Kevin and I are married, your adoption should be on the fast track."

Officially, the social worker said it made no difference. Off the record, she said Kevin should provide a steadying influence.

For once I'd kept my mouth shut. I wasn't about to rock the adoption boat now. Besides, what can I say? Everyone loves Kevin.

Kevin put his new keyring in his pocket. "From now on, I'll deal with the case worker and the bureaucratic rules."

I threw my arms around him. "My hero. I love you even more than I did a minute ago. That is such a relief."

I barely had time to get settled at the kitchen table and absorb the good news, when Mrs. C sailed in. She took up her favorite spot at the kitchen island. She'd changed out of her feathered slippers and wedding outfit. "Would anyone like something to drink? Water? Iced tea? Lemonade?"

We all waved away the offer with thanks.

"Come on, luv." The older woman refused to give up. "You'll not refuse a nice hot cuppa, eh? I'll use the percolator."

There was nothing better for strong coffee than the old pot. The promise of a steaming cup undermined my will. I nodded, adding a tired smile.

Kevin shot me a sideways glance. "It's nice to have a maid to take care of things."

I chuckled. Having declared herself my maid last fall, the older woman constantly let herself into my loft and made herself breakfast. Okay, she also watched Marcus, did laundry, and helped with the occasional crossword puzzle. I refused to admit I didn't mind her company. Occasionally.

How her visits would work with Kevin in residence remained to be seen.

I looked at Kevin. A glowing sensation started in my stomach than spread through my veins. I felt a smile start. "Think of the money we're going to save on rent."

"You're such a romantic, Belden." His warm tone gave no hint of sarcasm.

Visions of dollar signs danced in my head. "In a few months, we could establish a solid toe-hold in the lower middle class."

"Moving on up." Kevin slapped the table. "If only Mr. Jefferson and Weezy could see us now."

Marcus pointed over his shoulder. "And our maid."

"A British one at that." Mrs. C gave a sniff of evident satisfaction. Then, she poured herself a cup of coffee, filled a mug for me, and shuffled to the table in her pink slippers. "Everything English is superior, don't you know?"

A chuckle escaped Kevin's lips then died. His gaze locked on the empty chair at the end of the table.

Rabi's chair.

The pointed reminder of his absence sobered me as well.

"Running makes Rabi look guilty." Marcus hadn't missed the undercurrent. "That's what the cops think."

To be fair, most people believe fleeing implies guilt. Although, I have, on occasion, avoided law enforcement while being completely innocent.

"Looks can deceive." Kevin spoke as a master grifter. "We know the truth. Rabi is innocent."

"He's a target." Marcus's voice was almost a whisper. Worry for Rabi's safety robbed the boy of his bravado. "We can't protect him from a killer we don't know."

"We *can* protect Rabi." Kevin put a hand on Marcus's knee. "If we kill him first."

Shock derailed my mind from my mouth. I stared at my new hubby trying to figure out what I'd just heard.

"Oh, bravo." Mrs. C beamed at Kevin. She reached into the over-sized bag and pulled out her knitting needles and yarn. Settling herself in the chair, she nodded at me with a conspiratorial air. "I've died more than once."

Even for her, that was a bizarre statement. That's when my brain freeze ended and the gears started clicking. "You want to fake Rabi's death."

My newly attained spouse shrugged. "It would ensure his safety."

Marcus's head nodded like a bobble headed doll gone wild. "It has to look good."

"We need a body." Mrs. C asked with over-the-top enthusiasm. "I happen to have an acquaintance who is an undertaker. I'm rather certain I could work something out with him."

Having the older woman in my life has changed the way I view every person I pass on the streets. Her innocent demeanor hides a knowledge of deceit and crime few would credit.

My son leaned so far forward he threated to fall off his chair. "We'd have to blow up the body. Rabi's too recognizable."

"Whoa!" I held up a hand. "Let's take a breath before we drag a dead body out of the grave."

"Robbing graves is very messy." Mrs. C's frown bordered on a glare. "We need the corpse before it's buried."

I didn't even pause for breath. I certainly didn't ask for details. "No corpses. Buried or otherwise. No dead bodies."

I ignored the multiple groans of disappointment. "Desecrating a dead body is a crime. Not to mention, I don't want to be involved with corpses."

Marcus looked as If I'd just given away his pet dog. "You love murders. You're great at them."

"Neither of those statements is true." He made it sound like I was the killer. "I like solving puzzles and I've solved a few murders. I want nothing to do with dead bodies."

Taking a deep breath, I put my hand on Kevin's arm. "I like the idea of keeping Rabi out of danger. I think it would be better if we focus on finding the murderer."

An overly innocent look appeared in the depths of my hubby's sapphire eyes. "If you're sure."

I shot him a mock glare. The entire scheme had been nothing more than a diversion for Mrs. C and Marcus.

"We could have gotten away with blowing up Rabi." Marcus shifted his under-sized frame. A coil of energy seemed to build around him. "But we can absolutely find the killer."

A slow fire kindled in my veins, fueled by the lure of solving the puzzle. "What do we know about these men?"

The boy pushed the laptop out of his way. "Emerson and Rabi served together. The other guys from the poker game were in Special Ops at different times."

"We need background." Rabi could have provided details, but we'd have to start without him.

Marcus's phone buzzed. He grabbed it with the speed of a striking cobra. "Rabi. 'Follow rules. Checked in with admin. CUS.'"

CUS in Rabi speak translates to See You Soon.

A slap rang out as my son bruised the table. "Awww, follow the rules and check in. He went to see the cops."

"As he should." I stabbed the table with my finger. Relief loosened my tight muscles. "You can't play fast and loose with a murder case."

"He won't be on the run." Mrs. C sounded relieved. "Good news, that. Even if they hold him, he'll be safely tucked away until we clear him."

I have to admit I hadn't seen Rabi going to the police station after he escaped from them. Where had he gone? I said the first words that came to mind. "Wilson has no more information now than he did this morning. Still not enough to charge him."

My reward for my unconsidered babble was the hope that lit my son's dark eyes. Who knew I could make sense when I disengaged my brain? Maybe I should do that more often.

"She's right." Kevin's certainty enticed Marcus out of his funk. "That means Rabi will be showing up as soon as he's done --"

A familiar, rhythmic knock sounded on the door.

A sigh of relief seemed to lift the mood of the room.

Marcus's eyes ignited like a hundred candles. "Rabi!"

7

---

11 Across; 6 Letters;
Clue: A reason, often hidden
Answer: Motive

The boy was off and running before I could blink. He threw open the door. His sigh of relief released the tension in his thin shoulders. "You're back."

Rabi stepped into the living room. His gaze rested on the boy he'd all but adopted. The corner of his mouth rose in a smile.

Marcus's knuckles bumped Rabi's much larger fist. "Where'd you go?"

I pushed back my chair and walked over to grab an extra coffee mug. "Let the man sit down first."

"The gang's together again." Marcus shut the door with a bang and locked it for good measure.

Kevin raised his cup as he and Rabi exchanged nods.

"It's a fine thing to see you." Mrs. C's British accent gave an extra lilt to her greeting.

I handed Rabi a cup full of hot, black coffee. "Welcome home, Rabi. Did you check in with the police?"

Best to know for sure if I had to hide a fugitive from the law.

He accepted my words with an understanding look and the cup with a grateful smile. "Glad to be here. Wilson cleared me."

Marcus hurried to sit at the table. "Where'd you go?"

Rabi stared into the depths of the steaming coffee. "Find Olsen. Emerson left to meet him."

My interest meter spiked. "Last I heard the police were still looking for him."

Rabi's stern expression eased. "Ask the right people."

And the police didn't know the right people.

Kevin leaned forward. "What did he say?"

Lines appeared on Rabi's brow. "They argued. He left Emerson alive."

Marcus edged closer to the table. "He could be lying."

"No." Rabi infused the single word with a wealth of disappointment. "Security guard, former Marine from VFW, saw Emerson after Olsen drove off."

Mrs. C groaned. "That would have been dead easy."

Kevin cast her a sardonic look as his fingers drummed on his cup. "We would still have needed evidence of Olsen's guilt."

"We'll figure it out." My boy-child spoke with absolute certainty. "Rabi can give us background on the accident victims."

"No." My strident tone drew all eyes to me. "I have spent enough time in this wedding dress. I'm done. I'm changing. Two minutes."

Marcus gritted his teeth. "Rabi can just tell us a few details. We won't discuss it."

"Yes, you will. I would." I retrieved the dressy sandals I'd kicked off. "Nobody moves."

The boy's brow furrowed. "None of us guys changed."

I included them all in a sweep of my hand. "You took off your jackets, your ties, and you've unbuttoned your shirts at the wrists and cuffs."

Rabi gave the boy a wide-eyed look. "Don't cross mama."

"Two minutes." Kevin held out his hand. "We'll wait."

It was closer to ninety seconds. I threw the dress on my bed and slipped on the leggings and top I'd laid out for traveling to my honeymoon, then hurried to the kitchen.

Marcus gave Rabi a sharp nod as soon as I rounded the corner. "About time. Emerson said there were three accidents. Fleming and who else? Spill, dude."

The lean black man took a sip of coffee. His gaze had a distant air as if he were picturing a scene. His cup settled on the table without a sound. "Going to need a white board."

Marcus's eyes brightened. "Maybe two. We have three, no four victims."

Oh, the excitement of youth. He ran off to get his supplies from the closet. "We need names, background. The works."

Kevin gestured to Marcus. "You mentioned the poker games that started when? Year and a half ago? Then the organizer died and the rest of you fell out of touch."

"That's it." Rabi's tone sounded final.

My blood pressure shot into the stratosphere. "I'm supposed to solve a murder with a 'that's it'? Spill."

The man blinked as I smacked the table half-a-dozen times.

"I'd start talking," Kevin advised. "But that's me."

Rabi dipped his head, possibly to hide a smile. "Deighton, the organizer, died last year. I attended. Emerson, off and on. Politics. Lance Fleming and Kyle White came from out of town. Miles Redmond lived in a cabin in the hills. They always came to the poker games."

Kevin spun a spoon on his fingers at high speed. "Those last three died in accidents?"

Rabi nodded.

"We'll need police reports for their deaths, also any motives for murder. Friends. Relatives." I made the list automatically. "I can do background checks. Do you know where the supposed accidents took place?"

Rabi's long-fingered hands tightened on his cup as he stared into the depths of his coffee.

I set my mug down with a thud. Too abrupt? Sensitivity is not my strong suit.

As I opened my mouth, Rabi looked at me. His expression was studied. "Miles Redmond. Sixty-two. Retired lawyer. Having an affair. Disappeared at sea beginning of December. Body wasn't recovered."

I breathed easier at hearing Rabi's usual staccato delivery. "Passion. Fuel for revenge."

Rabi continued in his low drawl. "Lance Fleming. Sixty-six. Visiting his aunt in Lake Tahoe. One car accident, hairpin turn, mid-January. Kyle White. Forty-five. Fell while climbing at Red Rock. Early February."

"Red Rock is less than an hour south of Vegas." Kevin's gaze grew distant as he filled in his mental map. "All in state, except Redmond."

Marcus wrote the information on the whiteboard.

I eyed the names. "Emerson told you this before we got there?"

Rabi hesitated ever so slightly. "Pieced it together."

I filled in the words Rabi's sparse style left out. "Motives for murder? Trouble? Debt?"

Rabi looked up. "Fleming due to inherit from a wealthy aunt with two months to live. Survived him by three weeks. Her estranged daughter inherited."

I perked up. "Money is a solid motive."

Marcus chuckled as he filled in the information. "Money would be your motive for murder."

I stopped with my cup of coffee at my lips as I relented. "It might be in my top five."

A smile teased at Rabi's lips before he resumed his run down of the deaths. "White fell off a cliff. Ultra-marathoner, hundred-mile runs."

"That's crackers." Mrs. C let out a moan. "A hundred miles is a car ride, isn't it?"

"White pulled in sponsors." Rabi continued as if no one else had spoken. That's the best way to deal with our group, just carry on. "Planned to confront his partner about skimming money."

Marcus looked over his shoulder at me. "Embezzlement."

"Greed and passion can make people crazy." I watched the list grow longer. Lives reduced to a few lines on a whiteboard. An affair. Inheritance. Embezzlement. So little to leave behind. These men should have had years left. Whoever had cut them down would pay.

As I studied my friend, I felt guilty at my relief that he was alive. I was determined to see he remained that way.

Mrs. C scooted her chair closer. "Did you serve with any of this lot?"

Rabi met her gaze with a look of admiration. "I served with Emerson. He talked about Nevada. I came to visit."

Two survivors. Now, only one.

I looked at the multicolored whiteboard. Facts lay all around, but no clear leads. I was beginning to feel Rabi's frustration with Emerson's accusations. "Did Emerson have any idea who was behind the deaths?"

"He was upset." Rabi's understatement wrote off the murdered man's frenzied attack. "Blamed Olsen."

Who the security guard cleared.

Rabi was not the best client I'd ever dealt with. His quiet personality made getting dirt on anyone incredibly difficult.

I put myself in the killer's point of view. "The guy should frame Rabi."

Kevin's face creased in a slow smile. "Way to think like a murderer, Belden."

Marcus studied me closely. "You don't think the guy will kill Rabi?"

A hopeful note threaded through his voice despite his effort to remain professional.

I toyed with my coffee cup. "The other deaths have been ruled accidents. The cases are closed. Emerson's death is a high-profile murder investigation. The police will pursue leads until they have an arrest. I'd frame Rabi and walk away. But that's me and I'm not a killer."

Kevin's grin widened. "Thank goodness or we'd be part of a criminal enterprise."

Marcus smiled. "That'd be kind of cool."

Mrs. C broke off part of a muffin. "We commit enough crimes as it is, don't we? And we're working for bobbies."

"Let's get back to the case." I corralled the wandering discussion. "Crawford promised to check on the ME's report for the cause of death. Drowning versus skull fracture."

Kevin tapped his spoon on the table like a tap dancer doing a routine. "Best keep the accident reports close to home. Sooner is best."

Mrs. C waved her hand. It was like sitting with a five-year-old who had the correct answer. "Do let me ferret them out. I have acquaintances, don't you know?"

Stanley Kowalski had nothing on this woman when it came to knowing people.

Marcus gave Kevin a flat stare as he pointed at the older woman. "Pick her."

"Mrs. C, you are absolutely the woman for the job." Kevin sounded as if she were the only one qualified. "Marcus, make a note on the whiteboard."

"On it." The boy busily made notes with a colored marker in his neat penmanship. "I'll call Crawford for the ME's report."

Kevin rapped his spoon on the table like a gavel. "Who is Olsen? What is he writing about that could have destroyed Emerson?"

Rabi's mouth settled in a hard line. "Investigative reporter. Believed Emerson took illegal campaign contributions."

That made me bolt upright. "He told you this?"

Rabi nodded. "Today."

I didn't waste time wondering why Olsen had been forthcoming. Rabi is hard to refuse. "Emerson announced his run for governor a year ago. Millions of dollars have been pouring into his campaign."

"Wait!" Marcus slapped the table. "Emerson said you betrayed him. You wouldn't do that."

"I forgot that part." I fisted my hands and shook them in the air. "I even wrote it down. Was this during your deployment together? I need details."

My peripheral vision caught Rabi's half-smile before he sobered. "Emerson was in eighteen months. Dozens of missions. Discharged a year early."

"Why?" The question came from Kevin.

"Drugs." Rabi paused. "Captain put medical problem in the record."

"Any issues on the missions?" I tried not to pounce, but self-control is taxing, and seriously over-rated.

Rabi met my gaze with an intense look.

"It's not ratting out a friend." Marcus spoke with years of street wisdom behind him. "We won't tell, but we can't let you get hurt."

His plaintive tone would have ripped out the thickest walls.

Rabi gave him a nod. "Emerson was a weekend user. Never on a mission."

"You and him?" I prompted. "Any special history?"

His nod had the air of a salute for making the connection. "Last mission. Blow a bridge to protect a village."

Marcus's gasp sounded clearly over the lean man's slow, deliberate drawl. "You were ten miles behind the lines. He's the one. That's why you didn't want to tell."

Rabi's gaze seemed to focus on a movie reel the rest of us couldn't see. "Marcus knows."

The man fell silent, looking as collected as always.

Marcus glanced around the table. "Rabi and the other guy, Emerson, tried to make it back to base. They snuck past patrols and mines and guerillas. Hid for days. Then they were ambushed. Killed eleven guys. Rabi took four bullets. A grenade went off. He was hurt bad."

Rabi popped a few mints into his mouth. "Didn't think I'd make it."

A sinking feeling filled my gut. I wanted to turn away from the train wreck. But I couldn't.

I know it was foolish. The decisions, failures, and triumphs of those days were etched in stone. Yet I sat here hoping this time there would be no lapse in judgment, courage, or brotherhood.

Marcus's voice marched steadily on, relaying the story.

"The other guy left Rabi behind the lines. Injured and alone." Marcus's voice held no recrimination, but a frown furrowed his brow. Loyalty told him that leaving a friend was wrong, especially his hero, Rabi, but the survivor in the boy had learned the save yourself lesson from the streets.

Life or death. It's a lesson not easily forgotten, even after years of being wrapped in the cocoon of his adopted family.

A sigh escaped my son's lips. "He took the food and the weapons. He made it back. Told them Rabi died. No one looked for him."

Rabi broke a green mint and ate half. "He had a wife and three sons waiting."

Kevin's eyebrow rose as he eyed Rabi. Yet his expression held more acceptance than surprise.

I felt like I'd been gut-punched hard enough to lose my breath. How could anyone accept, let alone forgive such a betrayal?

No one at the table spoke for a minute. There was nothing to say.

"Pressure." Was Rabi's only comment.

The single word drained my emotions as if a spigot had been loosed. Fear. Combat. Courage.

What did I know? What would I have done? Stayed? Left? I looked at Marcus. Would I honestly have stayed with a dying man to be captured or killed?

Rabi's expression remained calm. "Pulling back the patrols saved me."

That and crawling through dirt and hiding under bushes for seemingly endless days.

I turned to Kevin, who pulled his solemn gaze away

from Rabi. My husband wore a harder expression than usual. A muscle jumped in his jaw. What I saw in his eyes wasn't vengeance for Rabi's former comrade-in-arms, but self-blame for the people Kevin had helped his family betray.

He was looking at his own past littered with the broken dreams and shattered fortunes of his victims.

"What's past is past." My sharp tone underlined the cliché in an effort to silence yesterday's guilt. "It can't be changed. We deal with today."

It took Rabi's nod and Kevin's lopsided smile to release the pressure in my chest. My exhale held a trembling note. I don't do well with angsty introspection. Time to marshal our resources. "Was there trouble when you returned?"

Marcus shook his head so violently his hair flew around his face. "Emerson was discharged to the States. He got a Distinguished Service Medal."

"Did you set the record straight?" I asked Rabi.

The former Special Ops soldier blinked a few times. "Told 'em I was alive."

My mouth flapped open and shut. Typical. "I wouldn't have left it at that."

Kevin snorted with laughter.

I really wish my brain and mouth would communicate better. "So, Emerson was the hero which he capitalized into a successful political career."

"Which Olsen was about to destroy." Kevin eased forward, as alert as a jaguar on the hunt. "Who knew the truth?"

Rabi's gaze grew distant. "Captain. CIA, their mission."

Good. A trail to unravel. "The CIA would have their own records and reports."

Mrs. C's eyes brightened. "You can get a look at those, eh? You've got friends, am I right?"

Rabi met her gleaming gaze with a sphinxlike expression. "I know people."

He reached for his phone.

Kevin pointed at Marcus. "Find Olsen's past articles. How many are political?"

The boy attacked the keyboard with a vengeance. He circled the mouse wildly, clicking several times before his face exploded in a triumphant grin. "His articles are *all* political. Exposes in DC and all over the country."

"Olsen has a source." Kevin's long fingers tapped a rapid rhythm on the table. He met the other man's gaze. "You need to back off. He could make trouble if you confront him again. We'll hunt him down."

"What does Olsen look like?" I asked.

Marcus dove into the laptop. "I'll find a picture."

Rabi watched the boy's finger fly over the keyboard. "Five-nine. Straight brown hair. Tan. Slim. Late thirties."

My son spun the laptop around to show a picture of the man. "There he is."

"Good. For your next assignment." I pointed at my son. "Research the victims. Money. Marriages. Relations."

Marcus stabbed the air with a red marker. "What about my weekend? I had plans with Rabi."

Rabi's expression tightened.

With a killer that might be targeting Special Ops vets, Marcus staying at Rabi's place was more than I could allow.

The boy folded his arms across his chest. "I'm not staying with you two. You're too mushy. I need a break."

"You poor thing." I laid on the sarcasm with a ladle. I was ready for a break myself. I'd been planning on one.

Kevin's expression held even less sympathy. "We all had

other plans for tonight."

I pressed my lips together and put my hand over Kevin's.

"What am I, then?" Mrs. C scowled at the boy. "Day old kippers? I was promised two nights with the young prince, wasn't I?"

I'd almost forgotten the arrangements for Marcus during the honeymoon.

"You and Rabi can stay with me." Mrs. C's expression bloomed into a smile. "There's a new padded mattress in the guest bedroom and an air mattress from army surplus. I also found us an old black-and-white movie about giant ants."

Marcus did a jig. "Rabi can have the bed. I get an air mattress and a movie night."

Kevin faced Rabi. "Are the police following you?"

The other man nodded. "Personal escort. Out front."

My hubby tapped the table. "The new security system up and running?"

"Dandy. Marcus put in the updates." Mrs. C sipped her coffee. "Cameras. Alarms. All spot on."

Marcus leaned on the table. "Rabi will be safe here. We can hunker down all weekend."

"The media hasn't caught a whiff of Rabi. They'd eat this up." I met Kevin and Rabi's gaze, calculating the odds. "I don't see how any of you could be more secure."

Rabi sat back. "I'll stay with my two guards."

I felt guilty about the times Rabi had been pressed into service as a babysitter, but his combat experience gave him an edge Kevin or I didn't have. "Olsen's contact information?"

Rabi gave me a flat stare. "Hotel. Room number. Phone number. False name."

That's one thing Rabi and I have in common; neither of us leave the hunt or the puzzle unfinished.

8

---

41 Across; 6 Letters;
Clue: A person chosen as the object of attack
Answer: Target

"So, this is my wedding day." Holding hands with my newly minted husband, I strolled down a street in Langsdale. "Looking for a killer."

"On *our* wedding day, my wife." Kevin pulled me toward him and gave me a smoldering look. "It's fitting. It's justice."

I lost myself in his eyes. I released a long, slow breath. "I can live that, and you. Forever."

We were walking down what passed for a lower rent neighborhood in Langsdale. The outskirts of town, not far from my apartment if the truth be told, hosts an area far removed from the high-dollar world dedicated to tourists.

We'd been to Olsen's hotel, where he'd rented a room for the week. When Olsen didn't answer the call from the front desk, the woman spent a few minutes drowning in Kevin's gaze while he questioned her. Finally, she admitted Olsen had eaten several meals at a small café down the block.

So much for not ratting out hotel guests. Not that I blamed her. My man could sell ice in the Arctic. "I'm not waiting for Olsen to come back. I have too many threads and too many victims. I don't know where this case is going."

"You'll solve it." Kevin blew away my worries without hesitation. "You poke people. They react. Soon bullets are flying. We're breaking into places. The police are ticked off. Like all your cases."

I laughed at his teasing tone. "The action fix from these cases is why you don't miss scamming rich fools on the French Riviera. My murder and adultery cases keep you occupied."

"But it's you I love." He put his arm around me and pulled me close. I could feel his heart beating through our thin cotton shirts. "With you and Marcus in my life, a chicken farm in Nebraska would be exciting."

"Chickens? Nebras—-" My words were cut short when he lowered his lips to mine. I lost myself in the feel and the taste of him. The sun on my skin and the breeze that cooled my warm cheeks were background noise.

All too soon, he pulled away. I brushed my fingers through his jet-black curls and pulled him close for another kiss. Then, breathing a satisfied sigh, I gave a short nod. "I could do Nebraska and chickens in a pinch. With our family, nothing is boring."

"The café's ahead." Kevin swung me in the direction we'd been walking. "Let's go find our pigeon."

With Kevin holding the door behind me, I scanned the corner café. The place reminded me of the smalltown diners from my Kentucky childhood. An array of desserts in a glassed-in case drew my attention. Pies. Turtle brownies. Huge lemon bars. Crumbles of all kinds.

I nudged Kevin in the side. "We may as well eat while we wait, just to be sure we don't miss the man."

Rather than follow my gaze, Kevin squeezed my hand before responding with a grin and quip.

He'd spotted our prey. A hardness appeared in the depths of his eyes. An extra alertness no one else would notice. Rather than scan the restaurant myself, I kept my gaze straight ahead as I followed the hostess to our booth.

Under cover of taking my seat, I studied the small interior through my lashes. In the rear of the café, Olsen was settled in at a small table next to the wall.

His constantly moving gaze scanned the small café in between studying his phone.

I raised the menu and shifted so the waitress blocked me from Olsen's line of sight. Kevin was sitting with his back to the man, but the mirror behind the dessert case gave him a perfect view of the reporter.

By the time the waitress left, Olsen was typing furiously on his cell phone with a speed I marveled at. "How do people type on those tiny keyboards? He looks like he's writing an entire article."

Such are the musings of the PI as she starts her case. That and deciding which delectable dessert to order.

"He's waiting for someone," Kevin said.

"That means I stand a chance of finishing the piece of turtle cake with whipped cream that I plan to order." I caught the waitress's eye. When she walked away with the menus, I felt bereft of the cover.

Good thing our prey was still focused on his phone.

"I don't get it," I admitted. "Minutes ago, he was looking around. Now, he's lost in his phone."

Kevin slid his fingers along the condensation on his iced-tea glass. His eyes narrowed in thought. "He got a text his contact would be late. That's why he stopped looking."

"Who is he meeting?" Another contact would provide a new suspect. I was in desperate need of live bodies. "Everyone except Rabi is dead."

"We'll find out soon." Kevin was as focused as I'd ever seen him.

My brain felt like a in pinball play. "I hate stakeouts."

"Even if you have a fudge cake with caramel and whipped cream?" His words heralded the arrival of our waitress. She slid my plate in front of me without so much as a glance. Kevin received a smile, a soulful gaze, and, yes, her number on the bill.

"Seriously?" I tapped the offending piece of paper. I understood the attraction, but still... "I'm right here."

With Olsen involved with his phone, I drowned my outrage with a bite of deliciousness. "I can wait for Olsen's contact to arrive."

A jingle of bells announced another patron. A quick glance showed a thin figure in an over-sized navy-blue hoody. Ear buds in, sunglasses on, head down focused on the phone in his hand, the new arrival strode past the empty hostess's station.

I swallowed the remnants of my treat. "Could he be more obviously mysterious?"

Honestly, it was over the top.

The new arrival marched toward the restroom and the exit signs. Both hung over a corridor in the rear corner. The guy walked past empty tables, bopping away to music only he heard.

Kevin tracked the guy toward the back of the café. "A hoody in Nevada? That's not right—"

Olsen, texting with one hand, reached across the table for the napkin holder.

My brain started screaming.

Kevin was halfway to the back.

As Olsen shifted, he looked up.

Halfway to my feet, I heard three pops.

The reporter's eyes widened. His body jerked as he slipped out of the chair and hit the floor.

The shooter in the hoody didn't break stride. He walked down the hall and out the door.

Kevin was almost to Olsen.

I was hot on his heels. "Call 9-1-1! Get an ambulance."

In seconds I was standing over Olsen's prone body.

After a single glance, Kevin started toward the hall and the alley beyond.

I caught his shirt and planted my feet. "No! Not today. Give me this."

Kevin tried to pull out of my hold. "I'm going to--"

"It's my wedding day. He has a gun." I gestured wildly to the corridor. "Let me end the day a bride. I'll never be a wuss again. Just this once."

He met my gaze with a hard set to his jaw.

I'd gone too far. I'd come between him and a chance to save Rabi. Kevin rarely loses his cool. When he does, family and friends are the cause. Day one and I'm looking at our first blow-up as a married couple.

"Belden." Facing me, he stroked my cheek with a whisper soft touch of his fingers. "You're the only person in my life who has ever put me before a job."

I sighed in relief and caught his hand in mine. "Always and forever. I'm almost glad the guy's gone by now."

"What happened?" Olsen struggled to a sitting position.

I jumped back as the shooting victim spoke. My eyes searched for a bullet hole. "No blood."

Kevin kicked the chair aside. He pointed at the wall. Two bullet holes neatly placed within inches of each other where the reporter had been sitting. No sign of the third bullet. "He slipped off his chair. Convenient?"

Suspicious. Was Olsen *that* lucky? Was anyone? What was the man's role in this drama? Victim? Chorus? Conspirator?

Olsen looked up at us from the floor. "What's going on?"

The faint wail of sirens sliced across my jumpy nerves.

Police in resort towns are prompt. Which meant I only had minutes to deal with the reporter.

"Are you hurt?" I grabbed Olsen's collar, partially strangling him, and tried to yank him upright. "Stand up."

Kevin grabbed the other man with one hand, righted the chair, and planted a babbling Olsen in the seat.

"What happened?" the man looked at the circle of customers, then focused on me and Kevin. "I've seen you two before."

His words pulled up the memory of Emerson's death only hours ago. "You've got bullet holes in the wall and you want to play guess who?"

He raked a hand through his shoulder length brown hair. Wide eyes. Slack jaw. "I'm a bit rattled."

"It's been a rough day for a lot of people." I fought to gather my wits. The growing cry of police sirens hurried me along. "I'm Tracy Belden, a PI."

Olsen snapped his fingers. "You're the bride and groom from this morning."

Kevin crossed his arms across his chest managing to

look friendly and intimidating at the same time. "You crashed our wedding... and left a body behind."

The reporter's head snapped around as if it were on a rubber band. "No way. I barely escaped with my life."

9

38 Down; 6 Letters;
Clue: Alive; unharmed
Answer: Undead

"I thought Olsen was dead." I fisted my hands on my hips and glared at Detective Wilson. "I can't be blamed for him being alive. I'm not paying for the ambulance."

Wilson gave me an evil smile. "I'm putting you in my report as responsible for a false call."

I drew back to my full height. "I might have saved the guy's life. You should thank me."

"Olsen isn't even bleeding." Wilson thrust himself so far into my personal space I could smell the Mexican spices from my breakfast brunch. "You're messing in my case and I don't --"

"Ah-hah!" I shoved my finger under his nose. "You admit

this shooting is related to Emerson's murder. Which means someone besides Rabi is responsible."

Kevin, standing on the sidelines, gave Wilson a thumbs up. "Way to give her an opening."

Wilson shot him a long-suffering glare. Jaw tight. The red flush rose from his neck to his face. Yeah, I knew those signs. "I've got the governor, the mayor, my captain, and the press all screaming at me. Now, you're in my face everywhere I turn. I should have you arrested."

"For what?" I was in the right this time. I hadn't committed any crimes. "We just decided Rabi's not involved in Emerson's murder."

"I said no such thing." The detective stabbed his chest with a meaty finger. "I deal with facts, not speculation that happens to aid a friend."

"You've obviously missed the connection." I lowered my voice to a reasonable tone. "Let me explain."

I'd barely managed to get Olsen's contact information, a business card no less, when the police swept over the café with a determined efficiency.

Detective Wilson followed soon after. Now, I was helping him sort out the facts. At least that's the way I saw it. "Kevin and I are trying to help. We saw it all."

"You have no description of the assailant." Wilson pointed out with a hint of smugness.

"Not true." I may have raised my voice again. "Kevin gave you a description."

"Partial." Wilson cut me off. "You have no business interviewing Olsen."

"You couldn't even find him." I gestured at the now deserted soda fountain. "Besides, I can talk to anyone I want."

"You're leaving." Wilson took a lung full of air. "Don't question the shooting victim when you pass go."

"He's not a victim. He didn't get shot." I pointed to Olsen through the glass window of the café.

He was standing with the uniformed officers, chatting up a blond, white woman with her hair pulled back in a severe ponytail. She eyed him with as much interest as she would a garden slug, while her hand inched toward her taser.

"Olsen and I are good friends," I continued. "He was at my wedding."

Kevin coughed at this point. Could have been a snort, perhaps a laugh.

Wilson met my gaze for several, stark, silent seconds. He took a deep breath then deliberately faced Kevin. "I'm only going to speak with you from now on. You're obviously the reasonable person in this relationship."

He wasn't the first person who'd made this observation.

Kevin, exuding patience, focused on the detective.

"I have your statements." Wilson spoke in a calm, even tone. "If I have any questions, I'll contact you. For your own safety, I am telling you to stay out of this investigation. It could be dangerous for you or any. One. Else."

He aimed the last three words at me, along with a hard glare and a threatening tone. Then he faced Kevin again. "Go home. Stay home. Do not pass Go. Just leave."

At a call from one of the CSI officers, Wilson spun on his heel and strode toward the crime scene.

I so wanted to follow the man. I mean, it's a free country, right? Unfortunately, Kevin's hand on my arm propelled me toward the door.

I frowned, but didn't protest. Instead, I decided to mend

fences. I yelled over my shoulder. "When this is over, Wilson, I'll buy you a drink to calm your nerves."

"You owe me an entire pitcher, Tracy." Wilson's voice rang through the length of the small interior. "If I survive the investigation and if I don't throw you in jail."

I smiled at Kevin. "He wouldn't throw me in jail. We're buds. Besides, he has to catch me in the act."

Kevin opened the door and stepped into the sunny spring day. "A beautiful day for a wedding."

Olsen's shoulders tensed at the jingle of bells over the door rang out. His gaze shifted in our direction. Then, he turned his attention to the patrol officer

I met her gaze—Officer Shepperd, according to her nametag. "Detective Wilson said we could speak with Mr. Olsen."

She aimed a knowing look at me. "No, he didn't."

I shrugged. It was worth a try. "None of us are under arrest. So, you can't stop me from talking with him."

She cocked her head to one side and studied me. "No, I can't."

As she moved away, I held out my hand to stop her. "Are you taking him in for questioning? Or putting him into protective custody?"

Her ponytail shook as she shook her head. "No, to both. He refused."

As she moved away, Kevin and I faced the reporter.

Concern blanketed Kevin's expression. "Next time, the shooter will connect."

The reporter, like any male, waved away the caution. "I'll be fine. The guy was crazy."

"Is that why you're sweating?" I asked. "That's why you said Emerson went ballistic? Did he attack you? It could be a case of self-defense."

"You won't be safe on the streets any longer." Kevin stepped into the ring with perfect tag-team timing. "Emerson was worried about a killer. Now he's dead."

Olsen's eyes darted from the black and white patrol cars to the gaping crowd on the sidewalk, murmuring among themselves and pointing at him.

I followed his line of sight. "The murderer could be watching. Waiting to follow you."

The other man flinched as my words hit home like darts.

"No one knows what he looks like," I continued. "He could have ditched the cap and glasses. Put on a wig, he could pop you in the back and walk away like he did in the café."

Kevin nodded. "The shooter's professional."

I didn't take my eyes off Olsen. "By the time they find your body, your assassin will be in Buenos Aires."

The man smoothed his Hawaiian shirt with shaking hands. "I'm on assignment for my newspaper, researching an article. I haven't done anything. I don't know anything."

I was disappointed that he was going to be difficult, and worried he might get killed. "You've been investigating Emerson. Several of his friends, who were also veterans from Special Ops, have died under mysterious circumstances."

The reporter's eyes narrowed. "He was serious? This is legit? Emerson could be the victim of a serial killer. This story could be huge."

The man was unbelievable. I stepped closer. "The killer obviously thinks you're on his trail. He's going to try again. How long do you think you'll last?"

"You're saying I'm a target?" Olsen's head spun around. His wide-eyed gaze shot back and forth among the onlookers, trying to look in several directions at once. "What do you suggest? That I go with you so he can shoot all three of us?"

I grinned, letting my certainty show. "Nobody's going to follow us away from here. And if you talk to me, you won't be the only target."

Kevin tapped the guy's arm. "I'll drive."

Twenty minutes later, we were on our last circle of the city.

The reporter had collapsed in the luxurious backseat of the Great White Beast. Also known as Kevin's car, it's a 1967 pearly white Cadillac convertible he's buying from his mechanic on payments. He and Marcus loved the thing almost as much as they loved me.

The only good thing I had to say about it was that the bright red interior made it easier to spot from the spy satellites.

Between the smooth ride and the release from tension, Olsen practically fainted with relief. We hadn't discussed Emerson's medal, the supposed accidental deaths, or the murder.

I know, hard to believe it of me. I decided to let him stew. Then, when we arrived at our destination, I'd hit him hard.

"By the way," I shifted in my seat to face Kevin, lingering for a moment to study his profile. "Where are we going? Obviously not home."

Kevin shook his head. He kept his gaze glued to the road. "That would be the first place Wilson would look once he realizes you escaped with the alleged shooting victim."

I glanced over my shoulder, but Olsen's closed eyes didn't so much as twitch. "I thought of that angle. I also considered a dozen others."

"No doubt." Kevin chuckled. "I'm hoping I can stay off the suspect list."

"So far, but I'm keeping my eyes on you."

"We're going to the Salt Mines."

"I love their bruschetta." Not to mention a gorgeous, shaded patio with a panoramic view of the desert and the mountains.

Kevin shrugged. "It's the least I can do considering you're not getting a honeymoon. Did you call the rental?"

"Several times. We're still in negotiations." I put my head back and let the wind wash over me. The soft leather was the most luxurious ride in existence. I'd beat the truth out of Olsen when we arrived. For now, I was off the clock.

A short time later we were seated on the patio.

"Enjoying the view?" I raised my pomegranate smoothie and aimed my sweetest smile at the reporter sitting opposite me. Kevin sat on my right.

The balcony at the Salt Mines was everything I remembered. In the middle of a Friday afternoon, it was mostly deserted. The appetizers had yet to arrive, but they were worth the wait.

I leaned across the table. "If you don't start talking, you're not getting any food."

"Whoa." Kevin set down his iced coffee with a thud. He faced the other man with a horrorstruck expression. "Coming from her, that's harsh."

I pointed at the bright flowers on the Hawaiian shirt. "My friend is in trouble. You're my only lead. I plan to pull on you until something gives. There have been accidents. Deaths. Now, murder and attempted murder."

Olsen raised his glass. "You have a way with words. Have you done any public speaking?"

I folded my hands on the table. "You're doing a tell-all on Emerson. Illegal contributions? His war years? Talk."

"Here we are." The waitress's words put a hold on my

command. She delivered a large plate of bruschetta and an order of bacon-wrapped shrimp with a sweet chili dipping sauce.

Once assured of our continued happiness, she smiled, glanced at Kevin, and walked away.

When the reporter reached for a piece of crusty bread covered with soft mozzarella, fresh tomato, oil, salt and basil, I pulled both plates away.

He looked at me, first in surprise, then outrage.

I just shrugged. "Unless you talk, this is mine. I'll share with Kevin. The law says I have to as of ten o'clock this morning. Also, I love him. And... I like him. Not you."

Kevin laid out the small appetizer plates for me and him. When he handed one to the other man, I stopped him. "Nope. Nothing."

Kevin gave a silent whistle. "You better cooperate before she pitches you over the rail."

I fixed Olsen with a glare. "I'll give you ten seconds."

10

36 Across; 9 Letters;
Clue: Unidentified
Answer: Anonymous

Olsen's jaw tightened. His breath hissed out between his clenched teeth. He buried his head in his hands. "I have no idea what's going on."

Kevin pushed an appetizer plate toward the man. "Admitting ignorance is the first sign of wisdom."

I munched on a bite of bruschetta. "Fortune cookie?"

Kevin opted for a shrimp with a generous helping of sweet pepper sauce. "Grandma Feilen. Plan. Research. Execute. The basis for every successful scam."

Olsen straightened and took two bruschetta. "I finished an article on the Nevada legislature last month. I attended a fundraising dinner in Carson City to pick up dirt. That's where I overheard a comment about fishy money related to Edward Emerson's campaign."

Kevin's gaze flicked over the man. "Details."

Olsen shook his head. "Hunting down rumors is my job. I started checking on him, his staff, any and all accounts."

I nibbled at a shrimp while I followed the trail. "What did you find?"

"Enough to keep going, but nothing provable." Olsen gobbled down a piece of shrimp, then snagged another morsel. His near miss with death had not diminished his appetite.

I liked that about him, though little else.

He pointed his fork at me. "Interviewed the staff, starting with his executive assistant, Jocelyn Hopper. I wrote a few articles to cover the hotel bill. I was pushing his office manager, Helena Dayton, for a list of contributors and the amounts. When she stalled me, I scented blood."

I filed the names away, drawn into the story. "You insisted on a meeting with Emerson based on that?"

The reporter took a long drink of his sparkling cucumber water and met my gaze. "My research is private."

I reached for his plate. "I'm taking the food back."

His hand blocked his plate. "I found inconsistencies in the accounting. I kept digging."

"Can it." Kevin's steely tone stopped our petty battle. "You told Emerson you knew the truth about a medal he received during his military service. What do you know?"

Several heartbeats passed in silence broken by a buzzing from Kevin's phone. He scanned the message before showing me the readout.

From Rabi. "Olsen's father CIA. Robert Herrington."

I couldn't hide a smirk as I settled back in my seat. Different last names. No wonder no one made the connection. "Your dad still works for the CIA?"

The man did a classic double-take. "How did you know? You can't know that."

I loved seeing him squirm. "You have your sources. We have ours. You threatened to expose Emerson. Destroy him."

Olsen spread out his hands. "I publish the truth. The man left a comrade in the field."

"The soldier survived." Kevin attacked with the swiftness of a jungle panther. "He credited Emerson's actions with saving his life."

"Lies!" Olsen's gaze burned with the fire of a vigilante. He slapped the table. "Emerson was awarded a medal he didn't deserve. He built his political career as a war hero. Rabi owes the world the truth."

Both men half-rose out of their chairs.

"Enough!" I put one hand on Kevin's arm. I knew how far he would go to protect Rabi. My other hand I shoved in front of Olsen's nose. "Rabi doesn't owe anyone anything. You. Sit."

The man slowly sat down.

"Take a breath, boys." I had my own priority. "The man is dead. Rabi left Emerson alive and well this morning. Olsen, you were the last person seen with him."

Okay, so I took a little license with the facts. Olsen's wide-eyed, pale face was worth it.

"You're a better suspect than anyone else." I paused to let that sink in. "I'll deliver you to the police and testify against you."

Not that I had anything to say, but he didn't know that.

I took a deep breath and another piece of shrimp. "Convince me you left Emerson alive."

"The man could have killed me." Olsen splayed a hand on his chest. "I was almost a victim."

"You provoked him." My hubby's cold tone could have cut bone.

The other man met Kevin's gaze and for once someone decided I was the better option. He faced me. "I told Emerson the facts when I called. He demanded my source. I mentioned some poker buddies he met a few times last year."

I smacked the table with my fist. "You let him believe his friends betrayed him? You rat!"

The man would do anything for his story.

"Oh, boo-hoo, Mother Teresa." Olsen looked down his nose at me. "You haven't lied to solve a case? I don't think so, Pollyanna."

I clenched my jaw. Admittedly, I played fast and loose with facts thirty seconds ago. That was to catch a killer. This guy did it to sell stories.

Olsen flung his hands up in the air. "I asked him who would know other than his comrades, including Jack Rabi, who refused to return my calls or speak to me when I tracked him down."

"Why didn't you push Rabi into a corner?" The mockery in Kevin's voice was something I'd rarely heard.

The reporter opened his mouth, looked into Kevin's eyes, then turned to me. "Emerson was berserk in the garden. I thought if I kept him off balance, I'd get answers about the money or the medal or both. I didn't care which story I wrote."

What a shock.

Olsen continued with his version. "The man looked baffled when I mentioned the extra money on his books. He said his office staff and accountants took care of the funds. After that, he refused to talk about anything but my source for the medal story."

"Your father." I folded my arms across my chest. "Who's broken several oaths to further your career."

Real fear etched itself into the man's face for the first time. "This is the truth."

I swept my hand through the air. "Finish."

Olsen took a deep breath. "When we met in the garden, Emerson said he knew Rabi hadn't spoken to me. Then, out of nowhere, he accused me of killing his poker buddies. Stalking and murdering them."

He looked back and forth to Kevin and me, completely dumbstruck.

"What do you know about the men he mentioned?" I asked.

Olsen shrugged then shook his head. "The poker games came up in my research. Human interest detail. He and Rabi have gone to the VFW for years. Emerson not so much lately. The others were out of towners. They last met ten months ago."

I leaned over the table. "Did you contact those men? Talk to them? Follow them out of town?"

"I never met them or called them. I had no idea they were dead until this morning." The reporter shook his head at each accusation. He held up his phone. "From what I found since, they died in accidents. Although the timing and the connections make it suspicious."

I pointed my finger at his chest. "Did you attack Edward Emerson this morning?"

Olsen put out both hands. "Emerson was alive when I left. Rambling about those men getting killed. He was losing control. He threatened to call the police. He grabbed my jacket and demanded answers, said he'd kill me before I could kill him. I pushed him away and ran to my car."

Kevin, a keen profiler from his grifting days, had been studying the reporter.

I cast him a sideways glance but I didn't really need his confirmation. Olsen's panic was plain to see from his shaking hands to the sweat on his upper lip.

The reporter had gotten some small measure of what he deserved, but he hadn't killed Emerson or the other men.

Olsen leaned forward. "Rabi is the only one alive who knows the truth about the medal. Give me fifteen minutes with the man. Okay, five."

One hint of a story and the man goes from victim to newshound. I didn't bother to hide my disdain. He was hung up on Emerson's medal. "Did you see anyone else this morning? Maybe following Emerson or you? Listening to your conversation?"

Olsen shook his head. "I saw a few costumed members from the Jane Austin group in the distance. Emerson caught up to me in an open flat. There was no one close enough to hear what we discussed. Emerson was in my face. He kept his voice low even when he attacked me."

The two were seen together. Was that pertinent? "Where are you going from here?"

"Not your hotel," Kevin warned.

Olsen frowned. "I need my notes."

Kevin and I exchanged looks. "The hotel."

We spoke simultaneously.

"Don't worry," Olsen said. "No one knows where I'm staying."

"Your office? Your editor?" I dug for my credit card, thinking of my expense report. Then I remembered I wasn't working for Crawford. I wasn't getting paid. "We found you."

Okay, Rabi found him. Let's not split hairs.

The reporter called for the waiter. "I got this. Expenses."

Kevin brought the other man's arm down and slid several bills on the table. "Cash only. No phone calls except on a burner phone."

Olsen opened his mouth, the denial on his lips. Then, he slumped against the chair. "The killer's after me?"

"You just got shot at," I reminded him.

Had Emerson been killed as the next in the string with the Special Ops vets? If they hadn't met in ten months why kill them now? What secret was the murderer trying to bury?

Kevin tapped the table. "We need to stash you."

Several minutes later, Kevin exited the restaurant first. His scan of the parking lot may have fooled everyone else. In fact, he was cataloguing the cars and the people.

I took a look at the panoramic desert stretching to the ring of dusky purple mountains. The dark patches of scrub brush and cactus crisscrossed in the shadows, like this case.

Olsen worked double time to keep up with me and Kevin, but he never lagged. He flipped through his notebook.

Kevin glanced oh-so-casually over his shoulder. "Four deaths with no answers. No reason."

"They have to tie together." I assured him, and myself. "Like a crossword puzzle building on each clue. I have to ask the right questions."

Whatever those might be.

As for Olsen, I didn't trust him. But if I ignored the threat to his life, he could be the next to die.

When we arrived at the hotel, the receptionist assured him he'd had no visitors except Kevin and me.

"See? No problem." A hint of fear underlaid Olsen's attempt to brush off the danger as he unlocked his hotel room.

Kevin's long arm reached forward, stopping us from entering the room. He pushed open the door with the back of his hand.

I stood on my toes to look over Olsen's head.

"What the--?" the reporter grabbed his head with both hands.

Scattered papers lined the floor. A duffle bag lay crumpled on the rug. An overturned chair was beneath the window.

Olsen started forward. "My notes. My tablet."

Kevin pulled him back.

When Olsen started struggling, I stepped aside to dodge a flailing arm. "It's a crime scene. You have to report the break-in."

"Stay." Kevin's grip and expression remained unshaken. "What's done is done. The intruder's gone."

Olsen's outrage ran smack up against Kevin's steady blue gaze. The man pulled away. He yelled, stomped, cursed, and muttered under his breath. "If I'd known... No one said..."

I tried to listen but it was a rapid-fire diatribe. Finally, he wound down. "Olsen, call Wilson. He gave you his card."

Kevin looked at me with a puzzled expression. "You know Wilson's number."

"I already promised him one pitcher of drinks." He was bound to blame me for being here. So what if I ran off with his witness? "Hey, we don't know anything. How about we cut out?"

Kevin rolled his eyes.

For someone raised by international con artists, my husband is annoyingly law abiding.

For the record, Wilson wasn't happy. Olsen's notes and tablet were among the missing. Though he admitted he'd uploaded his information to the cloud. This time Wilson insisted on Olsen going to the station to give a statement, after which he would be in protective custody.

Kevin and I received another warning. Then we were ordered to go home and stay home.

This time it was Kevin who laughed. "No one believes that's going to happen."

We did go home. I opened the front door to find Marcus six inches from my nose. I caught my breath and stepped back. My heart raced with the shock of being ambushed. "Where were you going?"

"To get you. I saw Kevin's car." The boy gestured toward the kitchen windows overlooking the street. "What did you learn?"

I couldn't fault the boy's enthusiasm, but I needed to catch my breath and get a cup of coffee.

A quick scan showed Rabi nowhere in sight.

"Where's Rabi?" Kevin asked as he shut the door.

"Scouting the perimeter." Marcus ran to the kitchen table. "We have police reports on the deaths, thanks to Mrs. Colchester."

"It was nothing, ducks." The older woman looked up from the pages she was sorting through. "Very interesting reading. Have a sit and we'll thrash it out, eh?"

"Rabi should be back any minute." Marcus stood on tiptoes to check the street. He spun around and fixed his black eyes on me like a pair of lasers. "What did Olsen say?"

Kevin sat next to Mrs. C. His eyes were focused on the pages she was reading. "Let's wait for Rabi so we don't have to say it twice."

A stir of air echoed from the front door. By the time I looked, Rabi was halfway across the living room.

Marcus clapped his hands sharply. "The gang's all here. Let's get started."

I raised the coffee pot to Rabi. When he nodded, I poured him a cup. The tantalizing smell of hazelnut teased my nostrils. I carried both mugs to the table. "What do we know?"

"No." Marcus spread his hands over the pages. "Give your report first."

"You're a little dictator." I shot back but complied, starting with Olsen's amazing luck at not getting shot.

Mrs. C tsked at the mention of the gunman. "You do seem to attract violence, luv."

"She's a death magnet." Marcus's voice was a perfect imitation of a voice over for a horror movie.

I ignored my son's familiar accusation and faced Rabi. "Did Emerson ever speak of Jocelyn Hopper or Helena Dayton?"

"Met them at the VFW." Rabi issued the news with barely a blink. "He hired Jocelyn five years ago. Helena maybe ten."

"Do you know them from the VFW?" I pressed. "Talk to them?"

Rabi shrugged. "In passing."

Kevin wrapped up the rest of our day with news of the break-in at Olsen's hotel and our dismissal by Wilson. Then he held up his hand. "The rest of the reports can wait."

Marcus gasped. His expression froze in a look of horror.

"It's Friday, that's game night." Kevin's words cut across the boy's obvious disappointment. "We need to relax. Mrs. C has a soccer game to stream in her apartment. If she agrees, we move down there."

The words drained more tension from my body. The stiffness in Rabi's shoulders relaxed. Everyone seemed to breathe a sigh of relief.

"Grand idea, luv." The older woman beamed. "I can't miss watching the lads."

"That works." Marcus gathered up the paper on the table. "You two can read the reports, then we can put it all together while we play."

After a hectic day that saw my wedding upstaged by murder, Kevin's words breathed a sense of normalcy into my world. "Thank God, for game night. I'll order chicken dumplings and fresh biscuits from the Silver Strike Café."

Ordering out was an indulgence I saved for game night. Kevin and Rabi helped split the bill.

Rabi caught my attention. "My case. My tab."

"You sure?" My token protest was only for the record. Once Rabi offered, I knew the man would insist on paying.

After Rabi assured me he was sincere, I hit my speed dial for one of our favorite diners. It was one of a dozen eating places I had in my contacts. Other people have their priorities, I have mine.

My autopilot took over when the restaurant answered. The woman not only greeted me by name, she rattled off our regular order faster than I could. "It'll be ready in thirty minutes."

I opted for delivery. I found myself staring at the phone after she disconnected.

Mrs. C collected her knitting project. "I'll pop off and get me digs ready."

I felt better having Rabi with us. Though I wondered what protection the four of us would be against a killer who'd allegedly murdered four veterans.

I could only hope a pattern would develop from the accident reports or from the victims. Despite what I'd said earlier, the fact that the bodies led straight to Rabi never left me.

11

---

16 Down; 8 Letters;
Clue: A particular place
Answer: Location

Scrabble was one of my favorite games, but tonight I hadn't laid down any word longer than four letters. I was behind in the scoring and my tiles consisted of one vowel and six consonants.

Seated at Mrs. C's kitchen table, I tried to focus on possible words, but my brain kept bringing up pictures of the accident reports.

Tiles. Look at the tiles.

I blinked at the letters. CCIDNTZ.

"Accidents." The noise and light of a hundred fire crackers exploded in my brain. I touched the papers that had been pushed to one side. My hand clawed at the police reports as if I could absorb the facts through osmosis. My brain pictured the lists on the white boards.

"TR, you're wrinkling the reports." Marcus's protest was all but drowned out by the noise in my skull.

The hand I held up to silence him was shaking. I locked on the list of names, details, and deaths. "Accidents."

"Ooohh, she's on the scent." Looking up from the soccer match, Mrs. C's voice trilled in excitement. "She's like a pointer in the field, she is."

I pictured the bullet points from Marcus's carefully built list. "Passion. Money. Embezzlement."

Marcus glanced at Kevin, but my hubby continued staring at me. "Those guys were murdered. They had to be."

A black-and-white grid danced in my brain. Clues aligned on both sides, begging for attention.

"Location. Location. Location." I snapped my fingers in a rapid rhythm. "The victims were on vacation. Sailing. Visiting relatives. Rock climbing. The killer waited for the men to leave town."

"That's why the murders were spaced out." A gleam lit Kevin's eyes. "Someone made sure the authorities didn't tie these deaths together."

A picture formed in my mind. "Older men. Family spread out. No one pressed for an investigation."

Marcus slapped the wooden table with enough force to make me and the tiles jump. "The guy who organized the group died last year. They haven't had a poker game in months."

Mrs. C muted the commercial on the TV. "Emerson found out. The killer couldn't wait this time, could they?"

"Someone knew Emerson had tied the accidents together and come up with murder." I latched onto to that thread, hoping it would fire my synapses. "But why kill these men now?"

"Olsen was nosing around Emerson's office." My hubby

laid down five tiles, covering not only triple word but a double letter with a Q. "Digging into the records. Money gone awry. Could be what Olsen found was embezzlement."

"Which has nothing to do with the first three deaths." I groused. "But embezzlement would give Emerson's staff a motive for his murder."

"Did you tally Kevin's points? Add them in." Mrs. C waved a hand without taking her gaze off her beloved lads.

I shot the woman a useless frown before adding up the score.

Marcus shifted his tiles as he listened. "Someone on Emerson's staff is up to something illegal."

Excitement built in my veins as I completed my tally. "Motive. Means. Opportunity. Emerson's staff might have known about the meeting with Olsen and followed him."

Mrs. C kept one eye on the soccer match while following our theories. "The reporter lad's been shot at, then robbed. He's a target, isn't he?"

"Since he talked to Emerson." Marcus knelt on the chair. He spun his arm in a weird circle and pointed at Mrs. C.

I chewed my lip. The voices in my head were talking amongst themselves. "You're right. Olsen's troubles started after he was in the garden with Emerson."

My son's eyes sparked at my buy-in. He rested his chin in his hands, sliding a look sideways to Kevin. "It's the gut."

Kevin gave him a knowing wink.

I stared at the Scrabble board. A grid of intersecting paths. Somewhere the wrong paths crossed for Emerson and Olsen, but embezzlement didn't tie to the three earlier accidents. "We need to take a different path."

"Yes!" Mrs. C's raised fist seemed a bit over the top for my suggestion. Until a roar from the soccer game on the television resolved the matter. "Take 'em, lads!"

I shifted my gaze to my son. "We need intel on Emerson's campaign. The office. The personnel. If we find who killed Emerson, Rabi will be off the hook."

Marcus's straight black hair, spiked up from a shorter cut, gleamed under the dining room lights. "I'll dig up the dirt."

"Emerson was killed in town." The voice seemed to come from far away, though the words came from my own throat. "People were close by. The body was discovered instantly. An investigation was inevitable."

Play on the table stopped as I outlined the facts. Even Mrs. C turned away from her game, though that doubtless had more to do with the commercial than my words.

"How does all that matter?" Marcus's demanding tone broke the lingering aura.

"I don't know," I admitted. "There are so many differences between the other deaths compared to Emerson's."

"No planning." Kevin spun the downward facing tiles in circles. He hadn't replenished the ones he'd used. The disdain in his tone for the lack of planning was clear.

His grifting relatives would have been equally appalled. The Feilens hadn't risen to the highest ranks of international con artists by overlooking the slightest detail.

"They panicked." Marcus's raised hand pointing at Kevin, held a tile which he added to the board. A four-letter word that also hit a triple word score. "Emerson talked to Rabi and Olsen. He was getting help."

"He argued with both of them. He was seen with them." I glared at the board while adding up the total. "How are you people doing this? Word games are my specialty."

Kevin patted my arm. "You have nothing to prove, even though you're losing."

His patronizing tone was only slightly softened by his teasing smile.

Marcus chuckled. "You're even behind Mrs. Colchester and she's not paying attention at all."

Now I was getting annoyed. "My brain is working on four murders. It's not concentrating."

"Yeah. Sure." Marcus's tone matched Kevin's. He slid a laughing glance my way.

I fought to maintain my glare, but the impish gleam in the young black eyes broke down my defenses as always. I burst out laughing. "Just you wait. I'll get you in the end."

My gaze turned to my tiles. While I struggled to focus on the letters, my words reverberated in my skull. "I'll get you" echoed back and forth, seeming to bounce down a long, dark tunnel toward the past.

I rested my arms on the table while I stared at the letters without seeing them. "The past. Revenge."

Rabi's dark gaze met mine.

"Well, duh." Marcus's tone held no respect for my revelation. "They knew each other in the past."

Kevin's gaze narrowed. "The victims met at the VFW, after they left the military."

"Location." I examined my earlier inspiration from another angle as I laid down my letters on the last triple word.

Marcus shrugged. "Meh."

When I poked him in the shoulder, his chuckle broke through.

I turned serious. "What if the motive for the three earlier deaths has to do with the VFW?"

"Excellent!" Mrs. C's enthusiasm seemed a bit much for my theory. She shook her raised fist at the screen. "That'll send them to the benches, won't it?"

I gritted my teeth and turned to Kevin. "I wish she'd quit doing that."

He was too busy laughing to respond.

The older woman repositioned herself to face the table. "I was listening to you, luv."

I tried to mask my disbelief.

Her pale green eyes met mine. "Location. The past. You want Marcus and I to toddle down to the VFW with Rabi and have a bite. Search the seams."

"I didn't say that." And what did search the seams, mean? I'd never heard that on any of the British mysteries or cooking shows I regularly watched.

"Reconnaissance in the field." Marcus pointed a finger at Mrs. C. "Good idea."

"It's still not what I said." I braced my hands on the table. "Is anyone listening to me?"

"You know what they say." Kevin covered my hand with his, sending warmth tingling through my veins. "If you have to ask, you know the answer."

I did know. The very old and the very young only listen when it serves them, and the two rogues at the table were masters at the art of selective hearing.

Mrs. C leaned toward Marcus. "Does tomorrow work for you, ducks?"

How could Saturday not work for him? He was twelve-years-old. My irritation rose as events barreled forward. That was ridiculous. I smiled at my childish reaction. "That's a perfect plan, Mrs. C."

Kevin shot me a secret smile. His fingers encompassed mine as the gleam in his eyes told me he'd read my thoughts.

With the planning taken out of my hands, I exchanged a look with Kevin. "Are we invited?"

"Who cares?" he asked. "I'm going."

"Tomorrow then, Rabi?" Mrs. C's invitation brought a nod from the only veteran at the table. "That's dandy. The VFW does an excellent weekend brunch."

Marcus rose up in his chair. "The VFW is a perfect place to look for someone who's taking out veterans. They have the knowledge and the experience to plan an attack."

A chilling reminder that we were hunting a killer.

54 Down; 9 Letters;
Clue: A person connected by blood or marriage
Answer: Relatives

S aturday morning, I woke to married life with my husband in my new bed. His eyes were closed but I knew he wasn't asleep. I rolled over and poked him in the shoulder.

With the speed of a striking cobra, he grabbed me in a tight embrace. After a lingering kiss, he stretched out, holding me close. "That was a wedding night worth waiting ten years for."

"I agree." I rested my head on his chest and met his gaze. "I love you and I want you to know that if we ever divorce, I'm keeping the bed."

He smiled and stroked my hair. "Good for you, but you're never getting rid of me."

"I'd never let you go." Life was good.

After we finally got up and drank our coffee in a glorious solitude, we collected Marcus, Mrs. C, and Rabi.

It was ten-thirty when we walked into the Langsdale VFW. Decades of combat experience were on full display. Older couples mixed with young families. The wooden tables that filled the spacious dining room were easily three-fourths occupied.

A few individuals sat at the polished bar that stretched along one side of the room. A steam table full of gleaming serving dishes filled the air with a number of intoxicating aromas.

My stomach woke up at the smells. "We should eat first. Then we can discuss strategy."

Marcus studied the array of food, then he scanned the table of desserts. "Absolutely."

Kevin rolled his eyes. "As if anyone believed you Beldens would miss a meal. I've never been with anyone else who actually ate a second breakfast outside of a Hobbit movie."

I squeezed his hand while I tapped my skull. "We need fuel for planning."

Rabi answered numerous waves and greetings with a silent nod as he led us across the narrow part of the room. A couple loners at the bar gave our party searching looks before nodding to Rabi. We settled at a round table in the corner, partially hidden by a carved wooden screen.

A curvaceous red head in her mid-fifties walked out of the back hall aimed directly at Rabi. The nearness of our table to the corridor meant few people had a view of her.

Rabi stepped closer to the wall, which hid him from the view on the main dining room.

The slight smile on the woman's lips didn't match the cool look in her eyes. "Rabi. I was hoping to see you."

Rabi's expression didn't change. No sign of welcome or hostility. "Helena."

Dayton. My blood zinged through my veins. Something told me Rabi had only mentioned her name so the rest of us could place her.

This was Emerson's office manager. Olsen had accused her of stalling in turning over the list of campaign contributions.

The woman stopped in front of Rabi. "I'm certain you're as devastated as the rest of us at this horrible tragedy. You and Edward served together. He spoke of the missions you went on together."

Really? That seemed out of character considering Emerson's record. How much did she know about Emerson's military record? Or Olsen's plan to expose the story behind the medal?

The woman prattled on. "He trusted you. I only hope his confidence wasn't misplaced."

And people think I'm tactless. Was she going for a shock effect or was she always this outspoken? She evidently knew about Emerson's meeting with Rabi. His presence at the garden had been kept out of the media reports of Emerson's death.

She paused for breath, possibly hoping for a response to her attack. She was met with stony silence.

Rabi rarely defended or explained his actions to anyone.

Helena's forced smile remained in place. "I didn't mean to accuse you of anything. I don't know what to think. Edward mentioned he was meeting with you but he wouldn't say why. He's been very agitated this last couple of weeks. I thought you might know what was behind it. Was it the reporter?"

So, the office manager could have been at the garden

also. If she was embezzling, she had a perfect opportunity to frame either Rabi or Olsen. Emerson argued with both men.

Without planning it, I found myself on my feet, facing Helena. "I'm Tracy Belden, a friend of Rabi's and a PI. I'm investigating Senator Emerson's murder. It would really help if you would tell me whether he told you or anyone else why he was meeting Rabi?"

Her still hostility was replaced with a business-like mask. "When I pressed him for an explanation, he stated it was related to a mission and he couldn't discuss it."

The frosty look she shot at Rabi placed the blame squarely on his shoulders.

"Is that all he said?" I pressed. "Was the meeting listed on his calendar?"

She hesitated for a heartbeat. Then her outrage burst open. "He blocked off the time with no explanation. Unavailable. He refused to discuss what was bothering him. I've been with him for years. It's part of my job and Jocelyn's to help with damage control. We can't do that properly without the facts."

I didn't want to go into detail about Olsen. "I've heard rumors of illegal campaign contributions. Is there any truth to it?"

"Of course not!" Outrage sparked in her eyes, but she kept her voice low. "The opposition candidate spread those vicious, untrue rumors. A reporter caught hold of it and decided to make a name for himself. I refused to pander to the slanderous accusations."

Instead, she'd refused Olsen's request and fed his suspicions. "Is any money missing? Has an audit been done?"

The smile slipped off her face. "Our financing is strictly monitored. We conduct audits regularly. No money is missing."

She shifted to face Rabi again. "If there's anything you need, let me or Jocelyn know."

Raising her chin, the woman turned and retraced her steps down the hall she'd come from.

Mrs. C watched the woman's exit with a jaundiced eye. "She's a bit off the rails, isn't she? Love or guilt most often to blame for that, eh?"

I nodded in agreement. Rabi and I were both seated by this time. "That about sums it up."

We fell silent as a well-practiced server, an older man who greeted Rabi and Marcus by name, brought our drinks and waved us toward the food.

"No waiting." A few minutes later, Marcus settled at the table with heaping mounds of food on his plate. Most of the portions were hidden by an obscene amount of gravy. "I love buffets. You don't have to choose one thing and they never run out of food. We should come here more often."

I tore my gaze away from the thick-cut bacon, buttery hashbrowns, and the scrambled eggs on my plate. "The waiter knew you by name. So do most of the regulars."

The boychild pointed his fork at me. "You need to get out more."

Mrs. C shuffled to the table in her pink slippers. "They have kippers."

She held out her plate as proof. A handful of steaming buttery fish sat amid a small mound of potatoes and sauerkraut or possibly spinach. It was some kind of creamed vegetable that I had no intention of putting on my plate.

She inhaled deeply before setting down her plate. "The spread is rather international. The chef comes from France, don't you know? I have it from one of the staff who worked with MI-6 years ago. Spent time in Russia and Korea. Married a woman from Carson City then settled here."

No wonder she had so many contacts. She'd been in the building ten minutes and she had the chef's life history.

"The men and women here served all over the world." Marcus spoke between bites. "Tons of different wars and battles. The stories are way interesting."

My boy-child had always been good at listening and connecting with others. Distracted by my thoughts, I almost missed the instant his eyes widened.

A smile touched the corners of his mouth. "The Riviera side of the family is back."

Shock rippled through my bones. He could only be referring to one pair, but...

"They couldn't," I sputtered. "They wouldn't."

Rabi's gaze followed Marcus's. The older man's expression remained unmoved by who he saw.

Kevin and I had our backs to the door. I met his equally shocked gaze. As we turned, a familiar voice flowed over the now silent dining hall.

"Does one actually *need* to have served in an official war to dine in your establishment?" Fedor twirled his cane before planting it on the floor with a thud. "Or is it sufficient to have done battle with authorities in several lands?"

Safina, whose long blond curls rippled over her shoulders, graced the bemused hostess with a charming, and even I had to admit, dazzling smile. "We have family over there. Would it be possible to join them?"

"This can't be good." Kevin's mutter only reached my ears.

He'd taken the words out of my mouth, but what could I say? They were *his* relatives. "At least I got the down payment back on the tent. The VFW is on its own."

Moments later our party had expanded by two. Drinks

were brought. Plates were filled. The virtues of the chef and the herring were extoled; again.

"Madame, you are spot on." Fedor pointed at the fish on his plate. "This dish rivals anything I've eaten in the Old World."

I glanced around at the varied assortment of people at our table. Judging by the glances sent out way, I wasn't the only one. Fortunately, the normal bustle and numerous conversations filled the hall with a steady thrum that covered individual comments.

Kevin greeted his sister and cousin with a friendly but subdued smile. "Staying in town?"

Marcus perked up immediately. "What about the family business?"

Safina, like a five-year-old on vacation, had gone instantly to the sweets. She forked off a morsel of a sticky pecan role dripping with sauce and melted butter. "The Riviera sortie is on hold."

Everyone at the table kept their voices pitched low. Thanks to our position in the corner, which put us at a slight distance from other diners, no one else could have heard what we were saying.

My son frowned over a forkful of mashed potatoes covered with cream gravy. "But you had it all planned."

"Mmmm," Safina chewed for a moment before responding. "Patience is a key factor. For success, all details have to align correctly or it's a no go."

Fedor nodded knowingly. "Timing is off. Money isn't there. The mark is late or early. It's very stressful."

My son rolled his eyes. He shot an accusing look at Kevin. "Did you pay them to say that?"

Fedor jerked his head at me. "Your mother and my cousin both threatened me at the reception."

"They would." Marcus grinned at me and Kevin. "You don't need to worry. I'm on the side of law and justice. It's way more fun than I thought. Our current mission is to clear Rabi. You can help."

"Whoa." I could have sworn I spoke out loud but no one even glanced my way.

Fedor straightened in his chair. "I have always wanted to be a police detective."

"You've played the part numerous times." Kevin reminded him. His expression remained calm.

"That was make believe." Fedor scoffed. "This is the real deal. Much higher stakes with your friend's freedom and honor at stake. I'm in."

"Me, too." Safina's chocolate brown eyes oozed sincerity. "It was fun at the reception."

Marcus's expression grew solemn. "You have to behave. Rabi's family."

For the first time since I'd met him, what seemed to be a sincere emotion softened Fedor's twinkling gaze. "Family is everything. I promise to bring all my talents to bear."

"I would never dream of disappointing my newest nephew." Safina gave the boy a slow wink before shifting her gaze to Kevin. "It's also my chance to work with my brother again. I wouldn't miss it."

It took all my control to keep my trepidation hidden behind a neutral mask. While I honestly believed the two of them meant well, I didn't trust either of them. They didn't have Kevin's honest streak. They also had no idea what they were getting into with a murder investigation.

I bit my tongue and waited. Kevin was my ace in the hole. Neither of them would risk his disappointment or his anger.

My hubby had watched the exchange. Now, he tapped

his fork on his plate, three sharp raps. "Game rules. No side cons that interfere with the prize."

The stern words wove a spell around the Feilen cousins. Their shoulders relaxed and they seemed to settle into their skins.

Kevin's instructions were obviously code. No doubt used in family scams.

I took a deep breath as Safina raised a brow and looked at me. Doubts lingered, but given Kevin's temper and strength of character, I knew who would win in a clash with his relatives.

"The more the merrier," I said, "but this is not a game. There is no quit and there is no fail."

"Ooohh, I like it." Fedor shuddered. The ubiquitous smile bloomed again. "We're the good guys."

"Well, let's not go that far." My trepidation returned full force. How had I managed to sign onto such a wild ride as this was turning out to be?

I cast an apologetic look at Rabi.

He'd remained his usual silent self while the international con artists signed on to treat his life like an adventure.

Rabi held my gaze for a heartbeat then gave me a wink. His dark eyes shifted to Kevin with a reassuring nod.

The silent vote of approval eased my conscience.

"We got your back." Marcus smacked Rabi on the arm, diverting his attention. "Don't worry."

"Never do," was all Rabi said.

Safina raised a glass toward Rabi, her gaze solemn. "We will do our best for family. I promise you."

Fedor dabbed his mouth with a napkin. "Now, the juicy on-dits, please."

"Intel." Marcus corrected him, reverting to his preferred

military slang. "This is what know and what we're guessing."

Marcus leaned over and in a voice pitched so low I missed most of the details gave the salient facts. There were a few delays for refills and an aside into ingredients in the Hollandaise sauce, but it was fairly concise.

Well, for our squad it was concise.

Fedor drew designs on his plate as Marcus fell silent. "We are definitely shy on details."

Safina studied the room. "You need to know any out of the ordinary happenings about the people who frequent this place?"

"Gossip of any kind. Happenings. Big or little." I braced myself for a snide comment.

The younger woman fluffed her golden tresses with her fingers. "Leave it to me."

She stood and strolled to the gleaming bar. Literally, everyone in the place watched her cross the floor, stride by stride.

Astonished at her cooperation, my shocked gaze studied the mesmerized looks until I landed on Kevin's smiling expression.

He put his hand on my knee and leaned close, speaking in a soft tone. "Safina hates to lose. Once she commits, she's in it to the end. If there's anything hidden, she'll find it."

"I have trusted her with more than my life." Fedor serious tone made it clear he did not trust easily. "Neither man nor woman is immune to her charm."

A round of laughter answered his words. Safina stood at the bar surrounded by, not men, but two older women. With their heads bent together they cast flirtatious glances at the line of battered men sitting at the barstools. For an international con artist equally at home in Monte Carlo or at a five-star London hotel, she fit in perfectly in a worn-down VFW in a Nevada resort town.

"Poker, you say?" Fedor's narrowed gaze met Rabi's across the table. "The games would have been played in the evening or afternoon."

Rabi nodded. "Saturday evenings. Game tonight. Different crew."

A speculative gaze settled over the leprechaun-like features. "The evening and weekend staff of this establishment would be key."

I grimaced in the light of his dancing eyes. "Leave them some money."

Fedor cast me a stern glance that could have melted a glacier. "My dear cousin-in-law I can forgive such an offense only once and only because you should be on your honeymoon."

Marcus's laughter cut across the stern putdown. "You got nothing to teach him on setting up a mark."

"My apologies." I'd realized my mistake while I was still speaking. "I leave the set-up in the hands of professionals."

Kevin squeezed my hand. "You can still be the brains of the outfit, Belden."

"Pieces and puzzles and put togethers." An old saying from my great-aunt while I'd helped her patch together quilt pieces into a pattern. "There's no pattern yet. The accidents were out of town. Emerson was killed here after arguing with Olsen."

"She's thinking." Marcus explained to Fedor. Then slipping on an impish smile of his own, the boy pushed back his plate. "I need dessert."

Searching for a thread to connect the deaths, I took note of the scheming look in the boy's eyes as he walked away.

"I'd best keep an eye on the lad." Mrs. C pushed herself erect. "They do have quite the array of sweets."

I shook my head. "There go the foxes into the henhouse. We're not being subtle, are we?"

Kevin sputtered for one of the few times since I'd met him. "Subtle has never been a weapon in our arsenal. Results are what count."

Rabi contained his silent laughter. "I have faith."

Kevin's hand covered mine. "Tell me what revelation you had just now. I like how you arrive at the solutions."

Oh, that I could have as much confidence in my abilities as my sweet spouse. I grabbed the clues in one proverbial hand even as the structure of my mental crossword puzzle seemed to come undone.

"Different patterns for different quilts. You can't put them together." The words came from the homespun wisdom of my Kentucky upbringing, but they felt right the moment I uttered them. "We need to tie the accidents to a pattern or see if they stand on their own."

Like the others I pitched my voice low, making sure no one was about. Honestly, with the families and children and background buzz, I could barely hear myself.

Kevin's expression turned. "That's why we're here, to find a connection or eliminate it."

Glad for our silent communion, some of the tightness in my chest eased. I slapped the table in a soft rap. I turned to Rabi. "The poker games dropped off."

Rabi barely blinked as he silently agreed.

"Fleming and White lived in Carson City and Las Vegas. Redmond on the outskirts of Langsdale." My finger spun a circle to include the town. "You and Emerson hadn't met them for most of a year."

Kevin's fingers beat a rapid solo on the table. "Did they get together without you and Emerson?"

Rabi's features stiffened. "They had before."

My hand squeezed Kevin's forearm. I tried to contain my growing excitement. Facing Fedor, I locked on him. "Find out everything you can about any visits the accident victims made to town since last summer. Who met and when? Who else was here that might have seen them together?"

"Don't forget Emerson." Kevin interjected. "Was he with the dead men at any point? Cover the bases."

"The game is afoot, as my countryman would say." Fedor's features glowed. His gaze remained locked on me. "I can see why you sit at the center of this *familia*. You hold the spark that pierces the gloom. The puzzle solver. I would never have hit on that aspect of these murders."

His fanciful words set me back on my heels. I was saved from answering as our three field agents returned, one by one in rapid sequence.

The arrival of the wait staff to clear our table caused a delay in the next stage of planning. I was grateful for the chance to put my scattered thoughts in order.

My list of clues rearranged themselves in the strict lines. One puzzle? A bit larger perhaps, more scope. I was eager for information. "What do we know?"

A quick exchange of glances had Mrs. C graciously waving Safina to the front of the line. For Marcus, there was no question of putting himself ahead of his internationally polished, newly acquired aunt.

Safina tossed her locks over her shoulders as she forked off a nibble from a brownie with gooey pecan and caramel frosting. "The bartender is dating a member of Emerson's office staff, Richard Barsoom and Jocelyn Hopper."

I'd been concentrating on the trail of relationships so as

not to tangle them. The punchline hit me squarely between the eyes. I shot Safina a look of admiration.

She smirked in triumph. "They met here when she worked for a non-profit company that helped veterans file medical claims. She conducted seminars and free appointments in a small meeting room in the back."

Marcus rubbed his hands together. "Connections to the murder victim. Good job."

Safina tossed him a wink, before continuing. "Emerson hired Hopper away several years ago. Helena Dayton also worked here part-time. They both still live in town. Emerson keeps an office in Langsdale to be close to the donors. He's been traveling frequently this last year."

Kevin raised a brow. "Olsen interviewed both women. He was pushing Dayton for records."

I touched my hubby's arm. "New names for the suspect list."

He nodded to me before winking at his sister. "Details are everything."

The look she shared with Kevin and Fedor spoke to their shared history.

Safina smiled in complete communion with her twin. "The three accident victims have dropped in from time to time. They visited over the holidays. Thanksgiving. Christmas."

Fedor pointed at me. "They did get together on their own."

Safina cast me a measuring glance.

My confidence rose. Not to mention the fact that I'd managed to add to my sister-in-law's opinion of me.

Marcus perked up, grabbing onto the revelation. "They were here when Rabi wasn't? Does that mean he's not in danger?"

Kevin weighed the possibility. "As a suspect he's more valuable alive. The police have no other leads."

The boy nudged Rabi's arm. "Never thought it'd be good to be a murder suspect, did ya?"

Rabi chuckled. "Silver lining."

"New management was brought in four months ago." Mrs. C chewed slowly, letting the suspense rise. Giving way to the initial report in order to be the last was sometimes preferable. "There is speculation it was due to embezzlement."

I bit my lip to contain my excitement. "Sounds promising. The guys may have heard whispers or saw an exchange."

Kevin tilted his head to one side. "How much money?"

A mirror of his skepticism showed on Fedor and Safina's faces. We were talking about four deaths.

Mrs. C paused with a bite of crème brulé halfway to her mouth. "The annual budget is ten million. Rumor puts the take at several hundred thousand over several years."

Surprise marched around the table as the numbers sank in.

Fedor tapped his chin, then slipped away.

My eyes widened. "I had no idea this was such an expensive operation."

Rabi shrugged. "Wealthy donors. Write-offs. Adds up."

Kevin took a bite of my chocolate cake. "That's worth killing over."

"I'm in the poker game this evening." Fedor sat down with a note of triumph. "The visitors to this establishment touch on the most varied aspects of your fair town. Government. Police. Waste disposal. Construction. Real estate."

The hungry gleam of a shark on the hunt surfaced in

Safina's chocolate eyes. "I'll return tonight also. To root you on to victory."

A silent message passed between them.

A perfect tag team developed over the years.

I tamped down the unease that stirred in my belly. I'd learned over the years that wishing wouldn't change people or the world. Kevin had vouched for their good behavior. I would leave the situation in his hands.

My goal was to find a killer.

13

---

20 Down; 6 Letters;
Clue: A legal union involving two people
Answer: Marriage

It was almost one o'clock on Saturday when Marcus, Kevin, and I walked into our loft apartment. The Feilen cousins planned to go to their five-star hotel, Rupert on the Mark, then on to a sweep of high-dollar boutiques. Following that, cocktails at a Galleria March, a city-wide affair involving wine and finger food at a series of art galleries.

Mrs. C had gone to her place for a lie-down. Rabi had stayed at the VFW. We'd promised to meet later.

As I crossed the threshold, I let out a sigh. With just the Belden Tanner family on hand, I could relax.

I chewed on the theory that the accidents were tied to an event Rabi hadn't been present for. That would explain why he was alive and possibly why Emerson was dead. With the next breath, I worried that if I were wrong, Rabi stood in the crosshairs of a murderer who'd killed three... possibly four times.

At the thought, two crossword grids popped into my mind. The larger puzzle was labeled Accidents. The smaller had the title of Emerson.

"I think she's turned off." Marcus walked up and poked me in the side. Laughing when I jumped, he sat on the sofa and pulled his laptop into position. "I turned her power button to on."

I realized I'd only advanced halfway into the living room, a bare six feet from the front door.

Kevin walked in from the kitchen and handed me a cup of coffee in a covered travel mug. Then he stretched out on our new sofa. A multi-sectional with matching ottomans that could be configured different ways.

Kevin's former roommate, Jimbo, had presented it to us as a wedding present. One of Jimbo's two jobs is delivery. This sofa had a tragic encounter with a black marker thanks to a four-year-old as it was unwrapped.

The family didn't want it. The store wouldn't take it back. So, Kevin and I inherited our first joint piece of furniture. It cost Jimbo nothing, but that was my kind of gift. Thanks to Marcus's artistic talents, the back of the sofa was now a fantasy scene of stark trees with flying dragons and a spaceship.

Kicking off my shoes, I sat between Kevin and Marcus. My hand trailed over the slate-blue suede like material. I sipped my coffee, relishing the dark roast flavor.

House rules. No drinking uncovered liquids on the new furniture.

I settled in with a deep sigh. "Rabi's safe. I'm turning my brain off and taking a break."

Kevin chuckled. "When do you ever turn you brain off?"

"You should nap." Marcus stared at the laptop as he gestured in my direction. "You're old and you've had a long day."

Kevin rolled his eyes. "I'll order a walker tomorrow."

My son seemed oblivious to the sarcasm. "I'm pulling up my search results on Olsen. I don't trust him."

"You don't even know him." My tone was sharper than usual. Perhaps because of the old person comment or perhaps because I was tired and I *was* getting old.

Kevin's hand enveloped mine. His understanding gaze took away my private recriminations.

I reached over and brushed my hand across Marcus's black hair.

Marcus's gaze remained on the monitor while his fingers flew across the keyboard. "You're annoyed because this case is kind of boring so far."

"Boring?" Kevin stirred out of his relaxed attitude. Propping himself up on his elbow. "What do you Beldens need for excitement? We had a murder at our wedding."

Marcus looked into the distance. "*The Case of the Murdered Wedding Guest*. Perry Mason."

"Emerson wasn't a guest," I protested. "This isn't a Perry Mason episode, and I am not upset that we haven't had a shootout."

"Olsen was shot at." Eyes agleam, Marcus returned his attention to the monitor. "But Olsen wasn't in Nevada when one of the accidents happened."

Obviously, the boy wasn't listening to me so I turned to Kevin. "He's your son."

Kevin eyed me over the rim of his travel mug. "Two days into the marriage and you're going to start that?"

I smiled and leaned against him.

Marcus's gasp cut off my comeback. His mouth was half open and his wide-eyed gaze was locked onto the laptop. "Olsen was in the army. He was a marksman."

I lunged for the laptop. "Let me see."

"Stop that!" Marcus held on with a white-knuckled grip and fought to yank it out of my hands. "House rules! No grabbing!"

We wrestled back and forth for a moment.

"Cool it!" Kevin's stern command brought instant stillness and silence.

I released my grip, chagrined at my reaction.

"You behave." Marcus shook a finger at me. "You know the rules."

I should. Marcus and I had created and agreed on the list shortly after he'd moved in with me. Kevin had helped since he'd been a part of the boy's life as long as I had.

"I over-reacted," I admitted. "I'm sorry. I shouldn't have grabbed your computer or yelled at you."

"I accept your apology. You're ol--"

"Do not go there." Kevin warned. "You're smarter than that."

Marcus stopped in mid-word, then continued without pause. "You've had a long week and you didn't get to go out of town."

He patted my back in sympathy.

"I miss my honeymoon." I stuck out my lower lip. It was whiny but come on. "The rental company hasn't agreed to my view yet, but I have the phone number for their president. I am still planning to go to Lake Tahoe."

"You will." Marcus's sympathy seemed a bit over-done. He leaned forward, looked at Kevin, and spoke *across* me. "I would not go away alone with her."

"Thanks for the warning," Kevin raised his cup to Marcus. "But I will risk it when the time comes."

"You married her," Marcus put the blame on Kevin's shoulders. "Good thing I was part of the deal."

"Absolutely," Kevin's look of amused affection was totally sincere.

I shook my head at my guys. "I might not have landed him without you."

"You wouldn't have gone on your date without me." My son gave me a smug smile. "You're welcome."

"All right, genius." Trying to hide a smile, I pointed at the screen. "Show us what you've got."

He scooched closer as Kevin leaned in from my right side. "From a guy Rabi knew."

Kevin's gaze flicked over the numbers. "Those are sniper quality."

Surprise rippled through me. Thanks to his relatives, his talents ranged from profiling, to card counting to preaching fire and brimstone, but this? "How do you know that?"

"Doesn't everyone?" Marcus asked with a note of disdain.

Kevin gave the boy a wink. "If you want to con a Russian gun runner who ran a slave labor prison in Siberia, you have to know what you're talking about."

Marcus's eyes widened. "Did he come after you?"

Kevin took a sip of coffee. "With missing money that only he had the code for, he had bigger problems."

Even now, the glimpse of the world my longtime best friend had grown up in managed to astound me

"Olsen's good." Kevin met my gaze with a cool nonchalance. "Good enough to have picked off the dead men from a good distance. He'd never have been suspected."

I tucked the thought away. Olsen's skill solved nothing. He couldn't have killed the accident victims or Emerson.

We lapsed into a comfortable silence. Marcus flipped through more reports. Kevin glanced through the paper, while I worked the crossword puzzle, in ink. I read a clue involving a steady relationship. Eight letters.

Answer: Marriage

Not always steady, countered my inner voice.

Thoughts ricocheted around my brain. Houses. Living together. Relationships. Trust. The connections pinged off my crossword grid and into the case. "Redmond was seeing a married woman."

Kevin glanced at his watch. "I just lost ten dollars to myself. Eight minutes without commenting on the case. I didn't think you were capable."

I gave him a flat stare. "I'm concentrating. Since Olsen's off the list, I need to look at other angles."

"Roxie texted that the ME won't have a final on the autopsy until tomorrow." A smile touched Kevin's mouth. "I know twenty-four hours is an eternity to someone with the patience of a mayfly. Try to bear-up."

I smiled at his teasing. "I'll check on Redmond's alleged affair. I have experience getting the dirt on cheating spouses. It shouldn't take much to confirm the facts."

"Like "The ABC Murders" by Agatha Christie." Marcus looked up from his laptop. "You have to check all the victims."

I tapped the paper with my pen. "I pulled in..."

That's when I saw the smug look in Kevin's gaze. "What do you know?"

He took a long drink of coffee with the speed of a turtle on downers. "Roxie called your phone when you were out of the room. She gave me the report on Fleming's niece."

"Why didn't you tell me?" I put the paper down and leaned forward. "What did she find? Talk."

"It slipped my mind." He put down the cup. "The estranged daughter who inherited from Fleming's aunt is raising three teenage siblings she adopted. She hasn't been out of Indiana for ten years and has neither the time, money, nor contacts to put a hit out on her uncle in Nevada. No odd calls. No missing money."

I filed away the bullet points. "Just as well. I'd hate to put such a shining soul into jail. Adopting three teenagers. Good grief."

Kevin folded up the paper. "Redmond?"

"The woman and her husband live in town." This part I'd already mapped out. "I've dug into my share of cheating spouses. It'll be easy."

At that moment, Marcus shut the laptop and set it on the coffee table. "We have to leave for the soccer game."

Kevin tapped his phone. "Got the directions."

I met two pairs of eyes, not bothering to mask my surprise. "I thought the exhibition game was next week."

"You're on honeymoon brain." Marcus excused my lapse. "Rabi's going to meet us there. Mrs. Colchester will ride with us."

I wondered at the Wi-Fi speed on a soccer field.

"You stay here." Marcus waved away my dilemma. "Checking on cheaters is boring. You do that. I can tell everyone at the game Kevin's officially my dad now."

"You're sure?" Soccer is actually one of my favorite sports to watch Marcus. His small frame and quickness give him an advantage he willingly exploits. I sit in the sun, drink coffee, and cheer.

The boy-child nodded. "Fill us in later. Come on."

The last was to Kevin who was already putting his cup in the sink. Kisses of farewell and in moments they were gone.

The silence was deafening. It was kind of weird to be alone. But my fingers itched to get started on Redmond's alleged affair. I had to find out who had killed these three men and why.

Because I still didn't know if Rabi was safe?

14

-----

53 Across; 8 Letters;
Clue: An unexpected event
Answer: Surprise

When Keven and Marcus returned at four-thirty with news of a victory, Redmond's affair was fact.

As Marcus ran upstairs to get cleaned up, he yelled that he was starving.

"So am I." I grabbed Kevin's arm. "I have a plan, but the hard part will be getting away from Marcus."

Make that impossible. Turns out, I couldn't shake him.

It was five o'clock when the boy settled himself in the backseat of Kevin's pearly white Cadillac, stroking the soft red leather. A long sigh escaped as he looked around the interior of the Great White Beast. "This car's community property now, hunh?"

My head jerked around to face him. "No!"

"Yes." Kevin answered in the same breath. "Equal shares, including the payment if I default."

Outrage electrified my entire body. "Then you better not miss a payment, mister, because I am not taking up the slack for this stolen vehicle."

"TR, don't say that." Marcus pulled himself forward as far as his seatbelt allowed. "This car is a part of the team. It's our mascot."

Kevin turned on the ignition. "It's family property and it's not stolen."

He's been making payments on it to his mechanic for several months. I maintain it will be reclaimed when the proper owners track it down. Privately, I have to admit I love the smooth ride.

Marcus poked me in the shoulder. "No more teasing. This is our first outing as a family. I can use it for my English assignment. That would impress my teacher and the social worker."

"A family outing where we track down a cheating spouse?" I gritted my teeth. "Do you want to get me fired from the motherhood gig?"

Marcus rolled his eyes. "I'll hit the high points. Going to dinner with the new husband. Visiting family friends. Blah. Blah. Blah."

Kevin gave a thumbs up as he pulled out onto a main street. "That's my boy. Clean it up and sell it twice."

Marcus all but danced in place. "That's straight from Grandma Feilen."

I couldn't help but grin when Kevin laughed.

He shrugged. "Those are her words."

"Don't think you two are going to gang up on me all the time." I pointed over my shoulder. "Make us look good."

"Always, TR." My son's promise came complete with a Boy Scout salute.

Casting aside the rosy frills of family outings, the plan was to track down Lance Norton, husband of Redmond's former lover, during a chicken dinner at a local fund raiser. His wife, Alice, was president of the PTA. I kid you not.

Kevin hit the gas and slid the long, heavy car in front of a truck that tried to box him in. "Safina texted. She and Fedor are following a lead."

"What?" the word exploded from the backseat.

Kevin swept a hand through the air. "No details."

Not knowing annoyed me. "They never reported in from last night's poker game. We need to get them in the fold."

"Pizza from La Casa's." Marcus's tone was filled with anticipation. "That'll get 'em."

A new worry vied for attention. "They won't try a side game?"

"Not while Rabi's under suspicion." Kevin's response was certain. "House rules."

Grandma Feilen evidently ruled with an iron hand, even from the other side of the Atlantic. That and Kevin's strength of character.

Noticing the landmarks flashing by, I figured I had ten minutes to review the plan. "We're looking for inside information. Norton has a clean record. No altercations. No complaints. Not even a traffic ticket."

Marcus pounded his fists on his thighs. "Maybe a short temper? I'll talk up the kids and keep my ears open."

Fifteen minutes later, we lined up in the queue and donated to the chicken fry so the school band could keep playing.

My stomach double clutched at the smell in the school cafeteria. "Cream gravy and mashed potatoes."

Once in line, Kevin pointed to the prepared plates of salad. "Gravy isn't recognized as a food group outside of the Belden household. Vegetables are a food group."

I dutifully took a salad.

Marcus pasted on his starving child expression and requested an extra helping of gravy.

The woman took one look at this slim frame and gave him a bowl full of the creamy liquid.

Kevin was still laughing when we sat down at a picnic type lunch table occupied by an older couple.

I'll skip the back and forth getting to know you portion of the evening. Our table buddies had no dirt on the Nortons. They did introduce us to the band director and two couples busy with the school.

The new group may have been under the mistaken belief that Kevin and I had money, were looking to enroll Marcus in the private school, or were willing to donate for a mid-year transfer. Take your pick.

Marcus disappeared into the crowd with the children of our new buddies.

Two hours later, we climbed into the Great White Beast. "The food was great and if we want to hand over ten thousand dollars we don't have, Marcus can start at his new school next month."

Kevin shut the door and started the car. "Who are Mike and Tiffany Smythe? You came up with those aliases pretty quick."

"And where is the address you wrote down?" Marcus asked.

"Mike Smythe is a computer nerd from my high-school who married the head cheerleader." I always like to have aliases at the ready. "Tiffany was pretty and perfect and took barrel racing trophies like they were candy."

Marcus's expression was full of sympathy. "Was she the mean girl in your school? Head of a clique who tormented you?"

I forced myself to be honest. "She was sweet to everyone. She was perfect. She never got in trouble. She never stumbled."

Laughter erupted from my son. "Unlike you."

I'd spent so much time in detention I could have recreated the room down to the smallest detail. "Tiffany doesn't know mean. But she and Mike have the money to donate if they so desired."

"They sound boring." Kevin leaned over and kissed my cheek. "Unlike you."

Warmth spread through my veins as my hubby put the car in gear and drove out of the parking lot.

"Besides, you have us," Marcus said. "That's better."

"Yes, it is, and I wouldn't change that for a million dollars." Satisfaction at my life filled me like warm honey.

Marcus's eyes widened. "Really? Not for a million dollars? What about ten million?"

I looked directly into his eyes. "Not for a hundred million. Money's not worth my family."

My reward was the smile on my son's face.

He folded his arms across his chest. "We're pretty cool."

"I agree." Kevin puffed out his chest. "We are the cool family on the block."

"Unfortunately, we didn't lock down any leads." I watched the sun dipping toward the mountain peaks surrounding Langsdale. Purple and orange streamers painted the sky. "Norton seems as clean as his record suggests. You pick up anything?"

Kevin shook his head in answer. His fingers tapped the steering wheel. "He's too contained. I don't trust perfect."

"That may explain why we suit so well." I put my hand on his shoulder. Then, I shifted sideways so I could see Marcus. "What's your report?"

"Better than yours." He let the gloating tone hang in the air. After a few seconds, Marcus put his arms straight out to his sides.

Kevin watched him in the rearview mirror. "What are you doing? Taking off?"

"Bingo." The boy clapped his hands once. "Norton got his solo pilot's license last summer. He took his family to San Francisco for their big Halloween bash."

"A plane." The facts opened up a wealth of questions. "Redmond's body was never found."

Kevin beat a fast solo on the steering wheel. "We need to know where Redmond kept his boat and if anyone saw him take it out the week he disappeared."

Marcus pounded his fist on the seat. "Did they know Redmond? How far out was the boat found?"

I searched my memory. "I don't remember those details."

My son rubbed his hands together. "I'll check the report when we get home."

Kevin pointed at the stretch of highway, lit by a symmetrical string of planted trees along the city streets. "We're almost there."

Ten minutes later, Marcus watched Kevin unlock the apartment door with the focus of a vulture eyeing a rabbit. "Hurry! Hurry!"

Kevin glanced at the boy then at me. "I love you both, but patience is a virtue the Beldens do not possess."

Once unlocked, Marcus flung open the door and bolted inside.

Kevin waved me through with a courtly gesture. "Happy honeymooning."

I opened the door, busily planning the steps to confirm Norton's whereabouts at the time of Redmond's disappearance.

"Where have you three been?" Mrs. C's British accent accused us all equally.

I had to stop in the doorway and count to ten. Her unexpected presence was like hitting a brick wall.

Kevin hugged me from behind with a welcoming warmth. "Would you like me to carry you over the threshold?"

I leaned against his muscular body for a heartbeat. "Let's save it for when we're alone."

I walked toward the kitchen where Mrs. C sat at the worn, wooden table.

Marcus stood over the older woman. "What's up? Where's Rabi?"

"Rabi ran an errand. No details." The woman spoke hurriedly, barely glancing at the boy before targeting me. "Crawford called two hours ago, don't you know? It's the autopsy report. Said he'd e-mail you. Sign on."

Her red-tipped, talon-like fingernail tapped the laptop with the rat-a-tat of a machine gun.

"And Kevin thinks I'm impatient," I muttered as I sat down. Part of my brain wondered where Rabi had gone and why.

"Hurry." Marcus's warm breath fanned my cheek.

I turned to face him and found myself literally nose to nose with the child. "Everyone is going to have to sit in their own chair during this session."

Kevin was trying and failing, to cover his laughter behind his hand. "I'll put on a pot of coffee."

Marcus rolled his eyes before grabbing a chair and dragging it beside mine. He plopped down and met my stare. "What? I'm in a separate chair."

"Barely." Kevin's amused tone sounded from the kitchen.

I gathered my focus and signed into my e-mail. Marcus's hand shot in from my left. I blocked it with a move from *The Karate Kid*. "I can do this myself."

Mrs. C tapped her instrumental creation on the table.

I clicked on the message. The subject was innocuous. The first line in the message was... "Water in the lungs."

Marcus gasped. "And a fractured skull."

Mrs. C's rhythm slowed.

Kevin set two mugs on the counter, waiting for the brew. His gaze held a thoughtful look. "Not a Special Ops style."

Marcus jerked as if he'd been shot. "That's right. Rabi wouldn't have done that."

I forced myself to look at it from the police's point of view. "If they were fighting and Emerson pulled away, he might have fallen on the rocks."

An image of the green and blue hued boulders in the pond stood in a stark accusation in my mind.

"No, way." Marcus swept away my version without hesitation. "Emerson couldn't break Rabi's grip."

The heavenly aroma of fresh coffee wafted in the air.

I breathed deeply. The very scent settled my nerves. With a renewed calm, I clicked on the attachment. The report opened to a stark form of a human body. Front and back. Arrows and x's marked the location of abrasions and contusions. Damage to the skull. Bruises on the throat.

"Mud on his shoes. Signs of a scuffle at the pond's edge. No clear foot prints." I read the details aloud for Kevin's benefit. He was the only one who wasn't crowded around the laptop.

Mrs. C had moved her chair to my right side as a matching bookend to Marcus on my left.

Kevin handed me a steaming cup. His gaze scanned the report in a three second review. "Bruises on the chest and face. That's from the fight with Rabi."

I pulled my attention from the hot coffee.

"Bruises on the back and neck. He was held under water. Murder." The words slipped past my lips. I pushed the laptop and the offending report away. "They have no proof it was Rabi."

Mrs. C shifted the laptop to face her. "No other suspects, ducks."

I raised my cup in acknowledgement. Always the realist.

Marcus joined her, reading the report over her shoulder.

Kevin took a sip, his calm gaze met mine over the rim of his mug. "Nothing matters but the end-game. You run the table or you don't. We'll find the killer."

Marcus popped up. "Rabi would have broken Emerson's neck and he's trained to hide the body."

I raked a hand through my short, straight hair. "Those facts won't put Rabi in a good light with the police."

"He's got a point." A mixture of interest colored Kevin's tone. "If Emerson's body wasn't found, there wouldn't have been an investigation. The killer was hurried and scared."

The wrinkles on Mrs. C's face deepened. "The attack was ill-considered and... unprofessional."

I found my hands had formed fists. This was ground we'd covered before. "There has to be a pattern I'm not seeing."

How much of my crossword grid would I have to sacrifice? I had questions aplenty, but no answers. "The right questions in the correct order. That's the only way to solve the puzzle."

Marcus gave a nod. "I have to update my board. That will make it clear."

Kevin set his coffee cup down. He watched the boy grab the colored markers. "That's asking a lot of a whiteboard."

"His version of my black and white grid." I followed Marcus's progress, hoping a pattern would leap out. But I was no wiser when he finished than I had been before. I thumped my coffee cup down, spattering a few drops on my fingers. "Redmond. We never checked for possible witnesses."

Marcus yelped and grabbed the accident report. "Redmond sailed out of Vallejo. Three witnesses saw a man of his description from a distance. His boat was found just past the Golden Gate."

I rested my hand on my chin. Too tired to take the bait.

Kevin's strong hands started massaging my shoulders. "Nothing solid to confirm it was Redmond who left on the boat."

Would it be wrong of me to ask how soon Mrs. C intended to run off with her charge?

Kevin's touch disappeared. He walked over and slipped the report out of Marcus's hand with a deft move. "Did you pack enough clothes to last through Monday?"

Marcus nodded. "Absolutely."

An electric jolt shot through my veins. Yes! Someone else was taking charge.

Kevin clapped his hands. "Enough investigating for the night. Tracy and I are honeymooning. You, Mrs. C, and Rabi can watch giant creatures attack civilization. We'll start again in the morning."

"Late morning." Finding the truth could wait a few hours. The threads that bound the players had lain buried for months already.

Now I could investigate Redmond's death. Where that would lead, I didn't know. Was there one killer or two? Whoever had tried to shoot Olsen was running scared.

Pressure had almost destroyed Emerson in the Gulf War. Hopefully, pressure would bring down his killer.

15

---

19 Down; 8 Letters;
Clue: A period of reduced activity
Answer: Downtime

Reality, like death, does not take a holiday. On Sunday morning I took a break from murder to work on the B&T Handyman side of our income. Kevin and my small business was growing steadily.

My hubby and I had had a leisurely breakfast before I called to ask if and when Marcus would be joining us. Mrs. C explained she'd forgotten the Sunday morning breakfast meeting of her knitting club. Marcus, she assured me was welcome.

Kevin and I beat out the knitting club. My son's new dad cooked him a plate of scrambled eggs while I nuked the sausage.

Marcus waved a forkful of cheesy eggs in Kevin's direction. "We eat way better since you live here."

I couldn't believe my ears. "He's lived here for two days."

Kevin laughed as he set the pan in the sink to soak. "I've also been cooking here for years, but thanks for the thought."

"We have two jobs scheduled to start Wednesday." I studied my spreadsheet. "We were supposed to be out of town until Monday. If we pick up the paint from the surplus store first thing tomorrow morning and do the prep work, we can get ahead of schedule."

Kevin touched my shoulder as he walked to his chair. "We'll head out after we drop Marcus off at school tomorrow."

The boy child pointed his fork at both of us. "Do not solve this case without me."

Kevin sat down and scanned the file over my shoulder. "I guarantee the case will not be solved while you're in school tomorrow."

Marcus hunched forward, staring lasers at me. "You can pull me out of class. I'm smart. I can catch up on any lessons."

"No one is taking you out of school for a case." Kevin interjected the words without looking up from a blueprint.

"Finish your breakfast." I turned my attention to the computer screen. I loved having Kevin here all the time to play tag with Marcus. Two against one, the odds were a little more even. "I have to arrange supplies."

Brick red paint on two walls with pale peach on the other two. I grimaced at the mental picture. Who does that?

Had the three accident victims known something?

I tried to focus on the business.

The paint warehouse usually had five-gallon buckets of white, gray, or cream that had been returned as surplus. We'd have to order the brick red color special. Wouldn't hurt to ask if they had some shade of red. Or we could color the white or cream and just pay for the mix.

Running for governor required a lot of travel. Perhaps to the area where his poker buddies lived. Had Emerson visited the other men at their homes for some reason? Rabi wouldn't have known.

Could they have threatened to expose Emerson's past? He killed them then someone else killed him in revenge?

I gritted my teeth while the wayward part of my mind ran into a back corner giggling.

Get an introduction to Emerson's staff through Rabi.

The completion date on the red/peach room was Wednesday morning. Two days? This was a huge project for us.

"That's not right." I pointed at the screen. "This wasn't the timeline we agreed to initially."

Kevin stared at me with a surprised expression.

"What did I miss?" I asked.

Marcus put his head in his hand. "Kevin mentioned that date five minutes ago. You were thinking about the case. Admit it."

"That is not a hanging offense." I drew myself up straighter. "For your information, I was concentrating."

Marcus folded his arms across his chest. "On the case."

"Maybe, for a few seconds," I admitted. "Mostly I was adding up the cost of red paint. Have you finished the work the teacher sent home for missing Friday?"

A smug grin covered the boy's face. "You're deflecting."

I'd accused him of the same thing only last week. I frowned at being caught out.

"That's what happens when you teach him new words." Kevin gave Marcus a wink. "Show me your homework. We can't work on the case twenty-four-seven."

He took off at a run.

I tapped the print out Kevin held in his hand. "I have to contact the company about this date."

In response, he flipped the page around so I could read it. It showed me agreeing to the quicker completion for a twenty percent increase on our fee.

"This is dated two days before our wedding." I grimaced. "I can't be held responsible."

"We can do it." Kevin put the readout down. "Tomorrow's an extra day. I'll get a couple of guys. Jimbo will help. Rabi took all week off to lay low."

Marcus thundered back in and plopped down in a chair, sending it skidding across the linoleum. He smacked his backpack on the table. "I can help paint. Take me out of school."

"Get your homework out." I looked at the specs for the job. "If we get white surplus, we can color it peach. The brick red is a problem."

Kevin reached across to take the papers Marcus held out. "The red will work the same way. Use the white surplus as the base. It'll save us hundreds of dollars buying it new and having a custom mix."

"I should've seen that." I could handle the business side of the... business. Kevin had practical experience. As I glanced at my laptop the homework papers crossed my line of vision. Paperwork. "You don't suppose Mrs. C knows anyone who could access the travel authorizations state senators have to file, do you?"

My guys exchanged knowing grins.

♦ ♦ ♦

LATE MORNING FADED, then it was lunch which eased into late afternoon. Mrs. C had toddled in ten minutes ago. We waited for Rabi to join us while we rehashed the case and the business of paying the rent.

"You need to make progress." Kevin rapped his knuckles on the table. "The guys and I can handle the paint job tomorrow."

I blinked. "I... are you sure? Missing the contracted date is a big penalty. We can't afford to--"

"Risk Rabi." Kevin inserted the words smoothly. His steady gaze met mine. "Family first."

I chewed my lip but my lungs loosened enough to fill with air. "Thank you, Grandma Feilen."

Kevin gave a decisive nod. "You work the case. I'll work the paint rollers. We'll make the deadline."

Marcus leaned on the back of a kitchen chair. "You need back-up, a wingman."

That boy does not know quit.

"You are going to school," I informed him in a steely tone.

"Not me." Marcus put a hand on his chest then gestured toward the door. "Rabi."

Stunned, I swiveled in my chair. Framed in the doorway, was the man in question. "Where did you come from? I only turned away for a few seconds."

"He's a ninja. Disappears in plain sight." My son flipped the colored markers in his fingers, in a move that was pure Kevin. "We need to reconnoiter. Where is the Riviera Division of the agency?"

"Reporting for duty." Safina delivered her response in an upper-crust accent as she marched into the living room with Fedor. "Wait until you hear what we found out."

My heart picked up speed at their self-satisfied expressions.

Marcus pumped his arms in the air. "Progress reports."

Mrs. C wiggled her fingers in the air. "Have we thought about dining options?"

Kevin made a show of checking the time. "That took longer than I thought, and it was non-Belden."

Marcus ran into the living room. "Go out or order in? You shouldn't have to cook on your honeymoon."

I rested my chin in my hand. "He means you, and I agree."

"I'm in with not cooking," Kevin admitted.

I pointed my phone at him before hitting a speed dial. "Let's do Italian tonight. La Casa's."

After confirming our usual two large combo pizzas plus salads with creamy Romano dressing, I added a treat for myself. "Pasta primavera with grilled chicken."

Kevin jerked a thumb in Fedor's direction. "Spaghetti Bolognese with mushrooms. Straight out of Milan."

Fedor gave an appreciative nod.

This was followed by a gesture to Safina. "Eggplant Parmesan with angel hair pasta."

I completed the order and waited for the total.

Fedor walked up to me, wiggling his hand for my phone. "I refuse to eat this meal with lemonade. I have my limits."

I listened as he discussed the options and his compliments on their excellent wine cellar. I groaned aloud as he ordered three different bottles of what I assumed was fine wine.

Fedor laughed at my pain. "I will reimburse you."

"My tab." Rabi inserted.

Relieved, I returned his smile and debated whether I

should issue a token protest, confident that Rabi would override my offer.

Rabi met my gaze, amusement danced in his black eyes. "I insist."

Marcus held out his hand to Fedor. "In that case, we're getting dessert."

I held up my hand to ward off this grab for goodies. "You can't take advantage of Rabi."

Despite my protests the phone was delivered with a flourish. I met the unconcerned gaze of my husband and threw up my hands. "I've lost control."

Furrows marred Kevin's brow. "When did you believe you had control?"

"Rabi doesn't care. We're saving his life." Marcus exchanged a nod with a completely relaxed Rabi. Then he smiled at Safina. "The cheesecake is homemade. Key lime."

Safina perked up and held up two fingers, lacquered with black-and-white stripes.

"Two," Marcus corrected. "Plus, two tiramisus."

He looked at me just as I licked my lips.

"We do need fuel," I admitted, caving.

"Piece of lemon cake and Italian wedding cake." He finished with a flourish. "In honor of Kevin and TR getting married on Friday. They had to miss their honeymoon to help Rabi out of trouble."

The last was dripping with tears. "She was crushed."

Kevin pulled his coffee cup away from his mouth and he still choked.

"Really? All the desserts?" Marcus's grin widened. "That's great. I'll tell her you said so. Thank you."

Marcus ended the call with a decisive hit on the screen. "Maria sends her congratulations and sympathy. No one should miss their honeymoon."

He started to hand me my phone, then delayed to bump fists with Fedor.

"You are a welcome addition to the Feilen clan," the older man acknowledged.

Tossing me the phone, my son glowed in triumph. "It's in the blood."

Safina threw him a kiss off her fingertips. "I couldn't have done better myself."

Moments later, we'd retired to the living room. With seven, the kitchen table was a bit crowded.

Kevin pulled me close for an instant. "Put the case on the back burner. You Beldens and your two stomachs need to relax."

While we waited for the delivery, the Feilen cousins, aided by Kevin, regaled us with tales of their international travels and cons.

To be fair, they did include the close calls, the very real danger of trying to separate the rich and sometimes criminal from their bank accounts. They seemed to have traveled the world.

Marcus, with his chin balanced on one fist, toyed with the remnants of his key-lime cheesecake. "You don't have a base? Someplace to go between cases?"

A home, perchance. A corner of the world to call your own. To close the door on outsiders. Surprise colored his tone. Having found his own family, our street urchin had lost his taste for wandering the wide world.

"Hmmm, not so much." Safina dismissed the idea with an almost distasteful tone. "We go anywhere and everywhere."

When several sharp raps sounded at the door, Marcus threw his markers onto the whiteboard holder. "Food's here."

I stood as the others did. Mrs. C and Safina moved toward the kitchen.

Rabi walked to the door with the boy.

I followed his progress, watching the choreography of plates and glasses and silverware. While part of me added up the tally of what the food had cost Rabi, the other part of me reverted to the ripples spreading from what had already been a complicated case.

With a jaunty air, Fedor waded into the fray. "I'll uncork the wine. Do lay out the food."

The stories of adventures continued, including several rather shocking tales from Mrs. C.

I listened with half-an-ear, joining in the laughter.

"You never reported on your findings." The words escaped from my lips, completely disjointed from the conversation. The delicious food had fueled my brain. "You said you had information."

I eyed the Feilen cousins with an accusatory stare.

"She's right." Marcus flung out his arm in my direction. He didn't even try to dampen the outrage he threw at his new relatives. "Nobody says nothing until I get my boards."

Rabi followed the boy into the living room.

"You two need lessons on crime reporting." Kevin waffled his finger back and forth in a mock condemnation. He nudged my arm. "Way to throw them under the bus, Belden."

I shrugged. "I didn't actually plan it."

My sweetie grinned. "I never thought you did."

He knows my lack of impulse control.

The whiteboards were set up in short order while we waited patiently.

Marcus rattled off the latest revelations. At the mention

of Redmond's affair and Norton's pilot license, Rabi's eyes narrowed.

"What about the poker game?" Marcus asked. "Did you win?"

"Losers gain more than winners in the information stakes." Fedor noted.

I sat up straighter, pulling away from Kevin's warmth.

Marcus picked up the red and purple markers and pointed at Safina. "Go."

"The gendarmes in the French prison were less intimidating." Safina perched like a queen on her throne. She smoothed her dress, then fluffed her hair into elegant curls.

The performance was so far outside my wheelhouse, I could only watch in fascination. My brain had half-a-dozen scenarios ready for the multiple theories of who killed who. I wanted answers, facts, anything.

"Several details." She splayed long shining nails on the table. When her gaze narrowed, I worried she'd found a flaw. Instead, her expression became serious. "Definite embezzlement. Small scale. Honestly, why bother?"

"The game." Kevin exchanged a knowing look with his sister. "See if you can."

She clicked her tongue in agreement. "Caught. Confronted. Paying it back."

My shoulders slumped. I was disappointed. "No motive."

"There is more." Safina scooted her chair closer to the table. "Rabi certainly knows the details, but a number of staff and visitors at the VFW are involved with Newman's Flight School."

Kevin stroked his chin. "They have a small airport to the east. They give sky-diving shows several times a year. That had to be where Norton got his pilot's license."

The flight school and skydiving were growing attractions in the city.

Safina looked like a cat who'd eaten the cream. "Helena Dayton, in Emerson's office, has a partial interest in the flight company. Her son is a pilot. He convinced her to invest. She's very involved. She and Jocelyn arrange picnics for the staff and customers from the VFW to watch the training jumps and practice runs. They go out at least once a month."

My mind busily mapped out the threads. "That tightens the web, but where does it lead? Did Helena need money to keep her flight company aloft?"

"Not my job." The other woman purred with a smug smile. She pointed a painted nail at me. "That's for you to unravel."

Fedor stared at the whiteboard. "Several bartenders skydive: Larry Ervine ex-con, Richard Barsoom veteran, Nick Phelps on parole."

"Barsoom and Phelps are into *something*." Safina jerked as if a current had been shot through her blood. Her bright eyes latched onto Kevin's. "Those boys have money. Larry wears designer threads. Barsoom has a new Corvette."

Kevin clicked his tongue. "A date for further details?"

"Couldn't get a nibble." His sister's eyes held a knowing look. "Phelps is gay. Barsoom has Jocelyn Hopper."

Rabi shifted forward, drawing all eyes. "Emerson's Chief of Staff. Several years. Trusted."

An aura of shock radiated from all corners of the room.

"And there is the knot that ties the strings together." Excitement filled my body. "Hopper and Dayton came from the VFW."

Fedor cocked his head to one side. "You have an amazing capacity for digging until you find the crux of the plot."

Marcus sat down. "Crossword puzzles only have one correct answer. It has to work from all angles."

I listened to him parrot my words back to me, still concentrating on the puzzle.

Kevin pushed back his plate. He tapped the table's edge with his fingers. "Olsen was digging into Emerson's accounting. He was shot at and robbed after he spoke to Emerson."

"Consciences trip up the guilty with amazing regularity." Fedor looked from Marcus to Kevin before settling on me. He flashed his leprechaun smile. "Not me, of course, but weaker souls will become desperate and dangerous as revelations appear to be closing in. Do be careful."

His concern touched me. I acknowledged his warning with a nod as I spread my arms to Rabi and Kevin. "Thank you. I have my protectors."

"I have no doubt of that." Fedor raised his glass of deep red wine in response.

Safina hooked an arm over the back corner of her chair. She licked her lips like a cat with cream. "What's your gambit? Do you need more background information?"

"I prefer a frontal assault." I held out my hand to forestall arguments. I locked gazes with Rabi. "Rabi has just lost an old comrade. Emerson's staff could hardly turn aside a grieving friend. How about it? You can get us in for a visit tomorrow morning, can't you?"

Rabi nodded. The stern lines on his face looked as if they were carved from granite. A stone wall couldn't turn him aside.

16

---

24 Across; 8 Letters;
Clue: Conflict among people hoping to achieve power
Answer: Politics

Monday morning broke with gray clouds massed over the craggy peaks surrounding Langsdale. As Rabi and I drove along the outskirts of the city the wind whipped the low-lying mist into tall ethereal pillars. Then the eerie creations writhed and danced across the sands.

It was one of the wild displays that only exist in the desert.

"Well, that's worth the trip no matter what happens." I felt amazingly at ease.

One fact had been added to our arsenal. Marcus had found a picture of Helena Dayton at a fund raiser dated the day Fleming died. She'd been at activities three days running.

I wasn't ruling out conspiracy, but for now Helena had been moved off the main suspect list. I had one aim today: confront Jocelyn Hopper. She was the next stop on this runaway train.

Fortunately, Rabi is not lightly turned aside. He'd cut through the red tape for a ten o'clock appointment.

The man isn't as talkative as Kevin. That worked for me. I let my brain toss clues and answers back and forth. My gaze tracked the pillars of mists melting and swirling on the sands like living things.

By the time we arrived at Emerson's Langsdale head-quarters, I was in attack mode. Eager for answers. Questions bubbled in my brain.

As we entered the outer office, a brunette in a deep blue dress and a matching jacket waved the receptionist aside and walked up to me and Rabi. "I'm Jocelyn Hopper."

I shook her extended hand and introduced myself. "You and Rabi must know each other from the VFW."

She shook Rabi's hand, smiling in the face of his sober expression. "I used to see him more frequently before taking this job. I definitely know his reputation. Senator Emerson spoke very highly of you, both your war record and your friendship."

Rabi acknowledged the comments with a silent nod.

Jocelyn's pleasant expression remained firmly in place. "Let me show you to our small meeting room."

I was too amped up for small talk. I didn't have the patience to try Safina's charm and smiles. I also didn't have her tools. I had my own.

Jocelyn led us to a room roughly twenty-five feet square. We sat at an artfully arranged sitting area. Chairs. Soft pillows. A sofa. Coffee table. "So, Ms. Belden, you're a PI?

First time I've met a real one. You look nothing like the TV version."

I had to laugh. "The TV versions can hardly be called PIs. Most cases are solved by research, not chases and gunfights."

Jocelyn shook her head. "You're pretty famous in Nevada for solving murders. I'm glad Rabi has someone with your experience investigating Senator Emerson's death."

Time to knock her off balance. "I have an incentive to find the killer. Your boss was murdered at my wedding and Rabi is the chief suspect. I don't want to start my marriage by losing one of my best friends."

Jocelyn's lips parted, then she pressed them together. "I don't know what I can do to help. I was crushed to hear of the senator's death. All of us were stunned. I don't know who would want to murder him."

I raised a brow. "Did Senator Emerson say anything to you about his meeting with the reporter? You'd been in contact with Jason Olsen, correct?"

"Yes." Her jaw tightened. "Mr. Olsen had the mistaken impression Senator Emerson had accepted illegal contributions."

I kept my gaze locked on hers. "As the Office Manager you have access to the funds and accounting records. Did you have an audit done?"

"All of the contributions we received are legal. We are scrupulous in following the law." Jocelyn straightened in her chair. She spoke in a tight voice as a red flush colored her cheeks. "We conduct internal audits monthly. The senator and I also agreed to have an outside firm review our accounting. The review was completed Friday. It proves we are innocent. Unfortunately..."

Her voice trailed away.

All for nothing now. Emerson was dead.

I stretched over the coffee table. "Did the senator blame you? Was there any history of funds being mishandled in your tenure?"

Jocelyn jerked as if I'd struck her. Anger marked her eyes at my attack.

No doubt security guards would have been called for my removal, except for my escort. Of course, without Rabi I wouldn't have been in the building, let alone sitting on this soft couch with fizzy water close at hand.

Jocelyn took a deep breath. She went from fury to icy politeness before my eyes. "I never did anything to put the senator's reputation at risk and he was completely honest. The senator trusted me."

I wondered what secrets her steely control hid. "What did the senator have to say about the accusations? How did he plan to deal with the bad press?"

The other woman shifted her coffee cup, gaining time. "The external audit would have countered Mr. Olsen's fraudulent accusations."

I pasted a puzzled expression on my face. "Then why did he meet the reporter in person? Why give any credence to a claim known to be false?"

Jocelyn's gaze went back and forth finally settling on a spot to her left. "I have no idea why Senator Emerson met Mr. Olsen. I was baffled when he agreed."

Unfortunately, I believed her. Admittedly, political staff members learn to lie without blinking, but sometimes they tell the truth.

I was hoping for an indication she knew about Olsen's plan to sabotage Emerson's record as a war hero. She'd disappointed me.

"Did Emerson meet with Miles Redmond, Kyle White,

or Lance Fleming when he traveled to Tahoe, Las Vegas or Carson City in the last six months?" I asked.

Jocelyn's brow furrowed. "If he did, he didn't mention it to me."

"They didn't play poker together?" I pushed harder. "You must have seen them at the VFW. Or heard talk that they'd been in town."

She exhaled slowly, before meeting my gaze. "I didn't track the senator's social life. I don't know when he last saw them."

"Did he mention their sudden deaths over the last few months?" I asked without pause.

"You're annoyingly unstoppable." Jocelyn straightened her jacket, as if readying for a non-existent TV reporter. "If you weren't on a mission to clear my boss's friend from a possible murder charge, I'd have you thrown out."

"You wouldn't have let me in the building." I cast aside her judgment. "Answer the question."

A stiffness appeared around her eyes and jaw. "The senator never mentioned their deaths."

Yet she didn't appear shocked. The media hadn't reported on the supposed accidents nor had they been connected publicly with Emerson's.

Jocelyn eyed me with a bemused expression. "Helena Dayton told me they had died. She keeps up to date with all the happenings at the VFW. They were involved in accidents, I believe."

My brain zipped around like a merry-go-round at full speed.

Jocelyn checked his watch. "Do you have any other questions? I am especially busy dismantling the office, Ms. Belden."

"Good for you. My gram promised that keeping busy would keep me out of trouble."

Jocelyn pressed her lips together. "It's not working for you, I see."

"Never did." I had to smile at her rejoinder. I wanted to close any possible loopholes. "Have the police contacted you?"

"They spoke to all of the office staff." Jocelyn inclined his head. "I've told them everything I can. They asked many of the same questions."

The only other trail I had led to... "You and Helena are still involved with the VFW. You arrange skydiving picnics at the local airport. Your boyfriend evidently enjoys the sport."

Jocelyn looked amused. "Yes, he does. Is that tied to Senator Emerson's somehow?"

"I don't know," I admitted. "But I'm going to find out. I'm also going to discover who murdered your boss."

The stiffness in her face melted around the edges. "At least your annoying persistence should prove useful for something."

17

20 Across; 7 Letters;
Clue: A thing or things to be chosen
Answer: Options

Rabi and I hooked up with Kevin by early afternoon. He was at the job with Jimbo and the rest of the guys he'd hired.

"The prep work is almost done." I looked around the spacious rec room. "We're going to make the deadline."

Dollar signs danced across my line of vision like a line of Rockettes.

"We?" Kevin, who'd been up since dawn taping and prepping, stared at me. "*We?*"

"We're a we." I tapped my chest. "I organize. You just do more of the physical labor. I'm willing to help."

"No, no." The response was immediate, coming from multiple sources in the room. "Please don't."

Kevin stirred a five-gallon bucket of paint. "Your reputation precedes you."

"We're good." Jimbo, a former college linebacker, hugged me from behind. "Great wedding. Up until the dead guy. You're looking good, but, please, don't paint. You're a danger."

"You let Rabi help." I pointed to where our friend had already grabbed a roller with an extender and was putting color on the far wall.

"He's of assistance." My hubby hefted the bucket with no visible effort and handed it to Jimbo, who lifted it with two fingers. "Your effort will eat into our profits and set back our timeline."

I pulled out my tablet. "I'll work the business side."

"In between working on the case." Kevin picked up a roller and started on a nearby wall. "How'd it go with Jocelyn Hopper?"

"This whole peach offset with burnt red on the walls works better than I thought. I like it."

Kevin glanced at me over his shoulder. "That bad?"

I let out a long, disappointed sigh. "Jocelyn and Helena are either not involved or one of them is the murderer."

Kevin grimaced in mock sympathy. "Is that your new plan? Accuse everyone who's tied to the case of being guilty?"

"For now, that's the plan." I took a seat at a folding table and chair set up in the room. "That way I can say I guessed the correct person."

I chased the questions for a few more rounds but got no farther. It was time to get back to checking the personal lives of the men. I needed to nail down Norton's movements during the time of Redmond's disappearance.

Putting the case on the back burner, I concentrated on

the business. An hour later, I was ready to quit. Rabi's help had pushed our completion of the job up by several hours. The guys were cleaning when I received a text from Marcus.

"Extra soccer practice tonight. Pizza party." I read the message aloud for Kevin and Rabi, not bothering to hide a groan. "This will take all night."

Kevin didn't look up from packing away supplies. "Were you planning on catching the killer without telling Marcus?"

I scoffed. "I made plans for us to go to the airstrip where the flight school is located."

Kevin snapped the lid on the bin before meeting my gaze. "Norton's guilty?"

"Or innocent." I put on my best pleading look. "You can drive the Great White Beast. What if we drop Mrs. C off at practice? She's from England. She can't get enough soccer."

Rabi packed a neatly folded tarp in another bin. "I'll take them. I like soccer. So does my police escort."

I grinned at the offer. "Perfect."

Kevin set his hands on the closed bin and drilled me with his gorgeous blue eyes. "Why does it have to be tonight?"

I grabbed my purse and slung it over my shoulder. "I may have called about flying lessons. Norton is free in three hours, after a flight with a student pilot. He's willing to answer any questions we have about how far those little planes can fly. As well as details about planning and reporting a flight."

Kevin continued to pack up while the other guys carried the bins and supplies to the truck. "You're planning to nail Norton to the wall if he knew about his wife and Redmond's affair."

"I'd like to accomplish something," I admitted. "You can buddy up to him."

A thoughtful expression came over my new hubby's face. "Fedor and Safina might be a better match."

"I like the idea." I pictured the pair, a charming young woman and an urbane continental gentleman. "Safina might get farther than my smash and grab. You and I can loiter nearby. See how he reacts."

The Feilen cousins leapt at the chance to help. They met us at a local restaurant to discuss the details over an early dinner.

As we entered the restaurant, Fedor flipped his hat off with a flick of his wrist. "I'm thinking a warring married couple. Safina flirty. Me jealous."

His whispered words barely carried to the four of us as the waiter led us to a table.

In no time at all, the waiter was fawning all over Safina. Throw in Kevin, and I had a front row seat to what a threatening weapon the trio's combined charm could be. Their good looks and distracting patter were enough to undermine the best intentions of the most cautious people.

Kevin covered my hand with his, sending warmth through my veins. His sardonic look once again anchored him and our decade-long friendship. This was the world he'd left behind.

Safina tossed her mane of golden curls over her shoulder. She raised a glass of sparkling champagne while gesturing to the ones in front of me and Kevin.

"A toast to my brother, who appears rapturously happy." She met Kevin's gaze with a look of open affection. "Having spent several days with your new family, I begin to understand why this lifestyle satisfies you."

"Thank you, sis." Kevin tipped his flute to her. The

exchange seemed to mark an end to the undeclared standoff between the Feilens.

I took a sip along with the others. The sparkling bubbles exploded in my mouth, leaving a sweetish, sour taste. Delicious. Now to business.

"And to Tracy."

Darn, I thought she was done. I met her gaze, my smiling mask firmly in place. This should interesting.

Amusement lurked in the depths of her gaze. "I will limit my observation to your obvious love for my brother. For that and for giving him a home and a family when he needed both, I will always be grateful."

I can't say I succeeded in hiding my surprise. As we all took another sip, I had no doubt that was the last restrained comment she would make about me.

That's okay. I didn't have to live with the in-laws. I just had to tolerate them on their visits.

"Now to business." Kevin set down the champagne with a note of finality. "Before Tracy explodes."

"The poker games." I pushed aside my own glass of sparkle and pointed at Fedor, sweeping Safina into the gesture. "Tell me everything you heard about the men who died. The staff. Any details we didn't cover before."

"Very focused." Fedor straightened the silk scarf tied around his neck. "You would be hard to pull into a game."

Kevin and Safina widened their eyes.

The comment and their reaction put me off stride. "What?"

Kevin studied his cousin. "Admitting defeat? You?"

"For the first time." Safina's chortle held a note of shock.

"Not defeat." Fedor held up a hand. "But age has brought wisdom on the point of diminishing returns. Tracy is the most on point person I have ever dealt with."

I drummed my fingers on the table. "And look where it's gotten me."

He sighed and refilled his flute. "If you won't be swayed by compliments, you've emptied my arsenal."

Amusement overcame my irritation. "I doubt that."

Safina twirled her glass in Fedor's direction. "The staff and customers at the VFW are very intertwined. They take gym classes together. The skydiving, as discussed. Know each other's lives. Kyle White visited frequently. Richard Barsoom and Nick Phelps took skydiving lessons with him. Maria the waitress took stock tips from White."

The comment struck Fedor with enough force to make him draw breath. On the point of speaking, he instead smiled at the waiter who delivered our appetizers.

I inhaled the aroma of shrimp smothered in Havarti cheese.

Kevin, ever gallant, gestured to me to take the first morsel. "For my bride, who missed her honeymoon to clear a friend of murder."

Fedor toyed with one of his smaller forks. "If I'm ever suspected of murder, I'm bringing you in to investigate."

My mouth watered as I spooned the gooey cheese onto my plate. "You'd better be innocent."

Safina's tinkling laughter sounded like water gurgling in a babbling brook. She drew the attention of several patrons. "Touché."

"What were you about to say?" Kevin stole my question as I munched on a morsel of deliciousness. He aimed the plate and the query at Fedor.

The leprechaun turned serious. "I was wondering if Barsoom had been the recipient of money tips also."

Safina shook her head. Her golden locks swung like rippling waves of wheat a subtle but eye-catching move.

"The stock tip bordered on insider trading. White made her promise to tell no one else."

"This is a small town, much like Monte Carlo." Fedor paused to raise a hand in greeting to someone behind me. The twinkling smile returned on command. "Charming couple. No need of stock tips. Old money."

I didn't ask. My brain capacity was consumed with keeping the victims, motives, and suspects straight. The threads had multiplied like rabbits in the spring.

"Lots of wealth walking the streets." The hunger in Fedor's tone matched mine when I was eyeing a sirloin, medium rare. He sighed as he returned his attention to our table. "According to Nick, Richard Barsoom was in desperate need of money all last year. Deep in debt to the wrong people."

I added a piece of shrimp to a bite of buttery garlic bread while I waited for the rest of the story. The Feilens evidently loved dragging out the show.

Kevin sipped champagne. A thoughtful expression crossed his face. "The bartender isn't one of our missing or dead."

"Point to the home team." Fedor struck his glass flute against Kevin's. "Barsoom's money troubles disappeared late summer or early autumn. During that period, Barsoom took up sky diving again. He bought a car rather than catch rides. He resumed his gambling weekends in Vegas."

"Follow the money." The quote fell from Safina's lips as if they were her first words, which they may have been.

I wiped my lips with my napkin. "Barsoom said nothing to explain his turn of fortune?"

"That is the most telling point of all." Fedor rubbed his hands together. "Who doesn't love to boast of windfalls?"

Well, grifters and con artists for one. But he was correct,

most people are rarely silent regarding money. "Did Nick ask him?"

Fedor shot me a wink. "Barsoom claimed a small loan coupled with a spectacular run at the tables in Vegas. If true, his strike came from the slot machines. Marcus could take this man in any gambling game that requires skill."

"Interesting." I pushed my appetizer plate aside as the waiter approached with a fully laden tray. "His silence is damning, but is it enough for murder?"

---

18

54 Across; 8 Letters;
Clue: A flying vehicle
Answer: Airplane

Safina and Fedor arrived five minutes after Kevin and I did. Right on cue, of course.

My hubby and I were discussing sightseeing flights with the man at the front desk. Not a pilot, he organized the schedules, repairs, fueling, and maintenance. His talkative nature worked to my advantage since Kevin and I needed an excuse to stay and overhear the Feilen's confrontation with Norton.

A Tuesday evening in early April was relatively slow for tourists so our guy had time to linger. When he offered to show me the differences between single and double engine planes, I took him up on it.

Kevin wandered to the opposite side of the hangar.

Norton greeted Safina and Fedor almost directly

between me and Kevin. Small talk. Smiles. Safina shot a stiff look at Fedor, her supposed husband. He dismissed her with a not quite hidden sneer. When Norton tried to smooth the waters, he found himself on the receiving end of Safina's guiles.

Between listening to my guide while keeping track of the Norton meeting, I was relieved when the bells chimed at the door. I happily excused my escort with a promise to wait for him.

"That's the thanks I get for trying to save our marriage." Safina shook with outrage.

"If you had the decency to stop eyeing every man you meet, we wouldn't have to go to marriage counseling." Fedor's low tone carried far enough to reach my ears. "Another waste of money you dreamed up."

The bombshell flung her hand in his face. "That's all that matters to you. Money. Getting ahead. If you were ever home, I wouldn't have to speak to someone so I don't die of loneliness in an empty house."

Norton held out his hands in appeal. "Let's calm down. Perhaps this isn't a good time."

Though I and Kevin were in position to hear them clearly, their voices didn't carry to the rest of the garage.

My escort, drawn to the tense voices, eyed the small trio. He met Norton's gaze, but the other man waved him away. Putting on a smile, my escort abandoned me to lead the latest customers outside.

I stepped behind a small plane while the cousins continued the play.

"It's never a good time with him." Safina picked up on Norton's last words. "He's consumed with work. I've spent my life trying to make him happy."

"Oh, please." Fedor's scathing tone put my back up. "All I've done has been for you."

The anger turned to hurt, raw and bleeding.

These two were good. Oscar. BAFTA. They could have commanded the stage.

Safina looked down her nose at him. "It's not enough. Neither are you."

With quivering lips, she managed a hard swallow. Then she turned on her heel. Every step she took was punctuated by the strike of her stilettos on the concrete floor.

We watched and listened, following her exit until she slammed the door.

I had to stop myself from applauding.

Norton stood dumbstruck.

"Hah!" Fedor's yell broke the spell. "Little does she know I have proof that will leave her all but penniless."

I wandered closer, step by step, unnoticed by the two men.

Norton tore his gaze from the door. "What?"

"I had a PI follow her." Fedor's gloating grin held an almost evil joy. "Pictures. Dates. Credit card receipts. The whole bit. It's hard to hide assignations."

Norton stiffened. His features turned rock hard. "Yes, it is, especially when they don't try."

Following instinct rather than a nonexistent plan, I walked forward slowly. A large part of one puzzle was falling into place. The clues at dinner. The relationships at the VFW. The isolation of the small airport.

Fedor caught my advance with his peripheral vision. His expression was puzzled, but he retreated from Norton's side.

I stopped a few feet away from the pilot. "Your wife didn't try to hide her affair, did she, Mr. Norton?"

Norton jumped, so consumed with the farce he'd

witnessed, that he'd lost track of his surroundings. "Wha— Who are you?"

"I'm a detective." That sounds much more official than PI and it's true. I detect. Is it my fault if people believe I'm with the police? "I'm helping Detective Wilson investigate a murder."

My interview. My interpretation. "Has he spoken with you?"

Norton retreated. "The police? Of course not."

I nodded. "He'll be contacting you. I came tonight to get a few facts straight."

Norton shot an accusing look at Fedor.

Kevin's cousin let his jaw drop open.

I could almost believe he'd never seen me before.

He held up both hands. "I didn't know anything about the police being here tonight."

True, since no one from the LPD was present.

I squared off with Norton, forcing him to face me. "What happened last November? Did Redmond come here? Did he think you didn't know who he was?"

The other man started to speak, then clenched his jaw. Anger blazed from his eyes.

I nodded, pretending he'd confirmed a theory. "You knew; you knew about him and the affair."

Norton straightened. He threw back his shoulders, finally gathering his wits. "None of this is true. You have no proof. Redmond disappeared while sailing outside of San Francisco."

A chink in his armor? "How do you know the details?"

Norton gave me a pitying look. "I watch the news. It's a small town."

"And you remember the death of a stranger several months later?" I stepped forward.

He shouldn't have come here, but then you had to dispose of the body."

Norton's gaze shifted back to the door. He seemed to be listening to that other confrontation. "He was leaving town. He lived alone. No one expected him back for ten days."

I slipped the wrench back onto a nearby table. "Your wife was out of town. You had a plane fueled up. No one would ever know he'd been here. Where did you dump the body?"

The man scowled. His chin jutted out.

The murderous glint in his eyes fizzled at the sound of Kevin's footsteps. Hubby stopped an arm's length away.

Norton's shoulders slumped. "I buried him at sea."

Kevin gestured to Fedor, now holding the phone. "Got it all."

"Are you Wilson? Her partner?" Norton shook off his confusion. "She didn't read me my rights. That's not legal. I want a lawyer."

Kevin shook his head. "I'm not Wilson."

"But he is my partner." Smiling at the double meaning, I pulled out my phone. "I'll call him."

Twenty drama-filled minutes later, Wilson arrived with the full CSI team in tow. You'd think he'd be happy. I delivered him a killer, but no.

He left Norton inside the hangar with his real partner. "You lied to him."

"Police lie all time." I shot back. "It's perfectly legal."

Wilson fisted his hands. His entire body shook. "You're not the police."

I came within inches of his nose. "I told him I was a detective which is true. Stretching the truth started with how long the bank and the hotels keep their security tapes, which you need to check on."

Wilson shook his finger at me. "Don't tell me my job, Tracy. I could arrest you right now."

"For what?" I fisted my hand on my hips. "Helping solve a homicide and letting you take the credit?"

Thankfully, a skinny, bespectacled white guy wearing a CSI bodysuit interrupted us. He tapped Wilson on the shoulder without blinking an eye at our yelling. "Luminol shows traces of blood on the floor and the cart. Should be enough for a match."

I waved my hand through the air. "You're welcome."

Wilson took a deep breath and pointed to the parking lot. "Leave."

"You want our statements in the morning?" I asked in a calm tone.

"I'm not talking to you anymore today." The police detective eyed me with a narrowed gaze. He looked around until he saw Kevin, standing with Safina and Fedor. "You all need to come to the station in the morning to give your statements. Check in at the main desk."

Kevin nodded. "Sure thing."

Wilson turned in the opposite direction and walked into the hangar without another word.

I waited until the door shut behind him before facing my hubby. "Well, that was rude."

Kevin choked back a laugh. "You think?"

I shared an understanding look with the man I loved and pasted on a serious expression. "We're both talking about Norton, correct?"

My hubby's smile widened. He clasped my hand and walked toward the car. "Let's go home."

Fedor and Safina fell in step with us.

Fedor gestured over his shoulder. "You are friends with this detective?"

"He'll calm down." I shrugged away his concern. "He'll get credit for solving a murder."

My arm linking me to Kevin stretched out. I stopped and looked to where he stood frozen.

A puzzled expression on his face. "*A murder.*"

Safina ran a hand through her curls. "I was wondering how this fit with the other supposed accidents."

Now my shoulders slumped. I'd been so busy fending off Norton then arguing with Wilson, I hadn't given one thought to the bigger picture.

Kevin stared at the horizon, putting the pieces together. "Norton only murdered Redmond."

We four stood in a rough diamond, all looking in. My gaze happened to fall on Fedor, though I wasn't really seeing him.

Fedor's leprechaun features settled into a frown. "I am completely amazed that you found a solution with so few pieces. Mine is a talent. Yours truly is a gift."

"Thanks for the compliment." I could only work up so much enthusiasm. The gulf between the high of unmasking Norton was replaced with the rapidly deepening pit beneath my feet. "This doesn't clear Rabi."

"Brick by brick." Kevin muttered, still staring over Safina's head toward the horizon. "Piece by piece."

I raised a brow to the cousins. "Grandma Feilen?"

They all nodded.

I forced myself to concentrate on the case, not the setback. "All puzzles have a solution. There is only one final answer for each question. This murder has to tie into the others. The pattern --"

"A witness." Kevin's voice over-rode mine. His certainty was reassuring and in hindsight, obvious. "Norton wasn't alone."

The thought galvanized me. "A murder that's hidden. The victim planned to be out of town. No one realized the death wasn't an accident. Someone else knew Norton killed Redmond. They used that pattern to kill White and Fleming."

I looked at the hangar where the police team worked with a ballet-like choreography. Tacked onto the other corner of the building was a door labeled, The Office. "Student pilots."

"No," Kevin rejected the idea. "They'd have been in the hangar with Norton and Redmond. Coming. Going. Refueling."

Safina gasped, drawing out attention.

Kevin and I turned as one.

His sister pointed to a field fifty yards away. "The skydiving classes have a shed for their equipment. They could have had one of their picnics to watch Richard and Nick and some of the veterans jump."

I groaned aloud. "There could have been a dozen people here."

Kevin shook our joined hands. "And you have to find out who, puzzle genius."

"The office." I gritted my teeth. My brain whirled while my black-and-white grids morphed and bled into new designs to match the twisting case. "You and Fedor keep Wilson occupied. I'm sure you can come up with something."

Kevin nodded. "You and Safina are going to check out classes?"

His sister fluffed her long tresses. "Will this mess up my hair?"

I tightened my grip on Kevin's hand for a heartbeat

before shaking loose. "Go get Wilson. We can't let him get there first. Safina, come on."

I wiggled my fingers at my sister-in-law and walked toward the far corner of the building with a determined stride.

"Can I be the annoying one, this time?" Fedor's question held a hint of sarcasm as we left them behind.

"Only if you're sure you pull it off." Kevin spoke in a mocking tone.

As if Kevin could ever be cast as the bad guy. It would take work for anyone to take umbrage with my man.

Safina clicked her tongue as the distance between us and the men diverged. "Do you have anything resembling a plan?"

Several tangents ricocheted in the back of my brain, like a pinball machine in play. "What do you think?"

She gave a long-suffering sigh. "That's what I was afraid of. How do manage to pull these things off?"

"It usually works out." Although at the moment, my mind was a blank canvas. I could only hope there was a masterpiece lurking rather than a fingerpainting by a five-year-old.

I marshalled the facts like soldiers. "Redmond was seen at the club on November thirtieth. According to Rabi, he was due to drive all day on December second. He had to stop here on the first. That's the schedule of classes, we need."

We reached the door of the office. I sailed through with her on my heels. "Hi, could you help us?"

The black-haired, white woman standing by a file cabinet greeted us with a gruff look and a frown. "What are you doing on the grounds so late? Are you the ones who called the cops?"

Safina put her hand over her heart. "I had nothing to do that. She did it."

Just like my own sister, she throws me under the bus.

"What's Norton done now?" The woman zeroed in on me like a dog eyeing a hungry steak. She slammed the file drawer shut and hurried over to join us at the main desk. "That hound. Cheating on his wife while he complains about her not loving him."

I let my jaw drop as her scratchy voice grated over my skin. Whatever sympathy I'd mustered for the man dropped to zero. "That rat!"

Irene, according to the name on the desk, moved her reading glasses to sit atop her flat, black curls. She licked her lips and waved toward the hangar. "A couple of the boys say he's been hiding money from her. How bad is his trouble?"

"Murder." Safina eyed the small office with a skeptical look. But her eyes gleamed when she walked to the desk. "Tracy got him to confess. She can give you all the dirt."

Irene rubbed her hands together. "I hope his wife gets it all now. Who'd he kill? The boyfriend? What's his name?"

"Redmond." I shot a nervous glance out the front window. No Wilson in sight, yet. "He confronted Norton last fall. Everyone thought he left town and drowned while sailing."

The dark-haired woman put a hand over her heart. Her eyes widened. "Did Norton kill him here?"

"In there, during an argument." I pointed toward the hangar. "How long have you worked here?"

The woman folded her arms across her chest. "Seven years. How did you get involved?"

I leaned over the desk. "I'm a PI. A friend of mine is

suspected of another murder. I'm trying to clear his name. I think Redmond's death might be related."

Irene's gaze flicked to Safina.

The blonde's smile held a wicked undercurrent. "I'm just along for the ride. I love to watch a professional in the act."

Her pointed look and skeptical tone spoke volumes.

The sound of raised voices outside left me no time to comment. "Do you know the file system? Can you access the schedules from last fall?"

"I re-organized this office from the ground up." A sly grin covered Irene face as she sat in her chair. "What dates do you need?"

"Redmond was seen on November thirtieth." My heart beat faster, success and failure stood at my shoulders. "I need a list of names from December first. Anyone who would have been on-site. Not just in the hanger."

The woman's fingers flew over the keyboard. She seemed to click and close several different sites before finding what she needed. Her gaze narrowed. "Two classes. Sky diving. Basics of flying."

Wilson's carrying bellow sounded through the thin walls.

I sucked in a breath. Not now. I was so close. "Can you print it?"

As I spoke the printer in the corner flared to life. It spat out two pages.

"Thank you." Raising my fists in triumph, I gave Irene a conspiratorial grin. Now to get out with the goods. I strode to the printer, but Safina beat me to it.

She folded the pages and flipped them out of sight with a skill to best any magician ever born. "You need deniability."

"Tracy!" Wilson was in rare form tonight.

I strode across the small office, rushing to meet him outside. As it was, I almost hit his nose with the screen door. "Have you seen Kevin? I got lost on my way to the car."

Wordlessly, the police detective pointed to the Caddy.

Kevin, leaning against it, gave a carefree wave.

When I started forward, Wilson barred my way with a meaty arm. "What did get from the office?"

"Nothing." I spat out the word. "Except that Norton's been cheating on his wife. Have either of these people ever heard of divorce? It's so much simpler than murder."

The man studied me through narrowed eyes. Three men in coveralls crossed behind Wilson. The one lagging behind wore a filthy baseball cap. I tracked their progress as Wilson's gaze raked my outfit up and down.

"Do you want to check me?" I held my arms out to my sides. My sleeveless, flowered blouse had no pockets. I raised the hem to show the band of my leggings, then spun around. "Nothing up my sleeves. You can check my purse."

Since it was a basically a wallet with a strap Wilson didn't take long. His frown got darker when he found nothing. With a last, silent glare, he dismissed me with a growl.

One point for deniability. It was almost painful to owe Safina, but I had to applaud her quick thinking. I kept my frown on and my steps dragging all the way to the car. I slumped in the front seat, sparing a glance at the office door.

Once out of sight, I all but bounced on the seat. I looked out the window for the Feilens' car.

Kevin dismissed my search in the same instant. "They're long gone."

"Safina has the lists of classes for that night." I was still excited at the win. "I assume she snuck out the back. I never saw her. I don't know how she got past Wilson."

"Safina walked past both of you." Kevin chuckled. "She was the mechanic wearing a baseball cap."

I didn't bother to hide my shock. "That was *her*? How'd she get all her hair in there?"

And that's how it's done. They got me when I was looking right at them.

"Did Wilson mention the other accidents?" Wilson was good at his job. If I could convince him of the big picture, his help would go a long way in solving the case.

Kevin's sideways glance brimmed with laughter. "The man did not share his investigative steps with me or Fedor."

I chuckled. "I'm surprised he didn't arrest you both."

An innocent expression crossed his face. "I didn't do anything except check on flight classes and watch you."

I reached over and squeezed his shoulder. "Redmond's death is accounted for. Now to see what those lists tell us about White and Fleming. They were both more involved with the VFW than I realized. I think that led to their deaths. But how? And why?"

19

---

26 Down; 8 Letters;
Clue: A plan of action designed to achieve a goal
Answer: Strategy

Marcus practically bowled me over when Kevin and I returned to the apartment.

The boy pasted himself to my side as I walked to the sofa to collapse and kick off my shoes.

"I've done all my homework." He spoke in an outraged tone as he confronted me. "I finished the book and wrote a report that isn't due for a week."

Kevin patted him on the back before sliding into the spot next to me. "I applaud your initiative."

Marcus pointed toward the kitchen. "It was Rabi's idea."

Conceived, no doubt, for the sake of sanity. When all else fails, distract the troops.

"Where have you been?" Marcus had learned interrogation techniques from Crawford, Rickson, and, yes, Wilson.

He stood over me, yielding not an inch. Stopping to draw breath, he held up a hand before either Kevin or I could answer. "I'll get the whiteboards."

Rabi entered at that moment carrying both of the items. "Got 'em."

"Ducks, I'm here." Mrs. C's voice and her distinctive shuffle sailed through the front door. She entered with her knitting bag slung over her arm. "I saw you arrive. Didn't want to miss any updates."

"Have a seat." Kevin pointed to her favorite chair. "We haven't said a word regarding the case."

Rabi, as usual, took up station by leaning against the archway which led to the kitchen.

Marcus picked up a marker. He perched on the edge of the ottoman. "Now. Talk."

A rambling, oft interrupted report followed. When all was said and done, a final pause left only the steady click of knitting needles in the air.

"That brings us back to the roster." I ended triumphantly. "Where are the cousins? Safina has the list."

Kevin favored me with a frown. "Oh, ye, of little faith."

He reached into his back jean pocket and pulled out two folded slips of paper.

I unfolded the pages to confirm they were the class rosters. My jaw dropped open. Even after all this time, his skills amazed me. "She didn't pass within six feet of you. How did you get this?"

Marcus gave me a pitying look. "TR, they're pros."

"I can't give away family secrets." Kevin spoke in a serious tone.

Marcus flipped a marker in the air. "Are they coming here? Do we have to wait for them?"

"Fedor and Safina had an engagement at the Regent, on the penthouse patio."

I looked up from the lists. "Are they planning something?"

"Only when they're breathing." Kevin spoke with calm certainty. "The fuse won't be lit until this case is put to bed. House rules. They will behave or they'll answer to me, and they know it."

Steel hardened his tone. Then, a lighter expression added a ray of humor to his eyes. "I could sic Grandma on them."

"Really?" That stunned me. "For grifting?"

"For the wrong priorities." Kevin spoke as if the difference was obvious. "Family first is what has kept the Feilens track record so successful."

"If they're not coming, we can get back to our case." Marcus pointed to the board. "Redmond's murder had nothing to do with the VFW or Olsen trying to expose Emerson."

Mrs. C peered at the board. "What does that leave?"

"There's the money angle." I sipped my coffee, studying the color-coded board. "Hopper and Dayton at Emerson's office were supposedly cleared by an audit. Barsoom and Phelps are well-to-do bartenders. I'm not taking anyone left alive off the suspect list."

"Wise move, luv." Mrs. C's accent gave the comment a bracing quality. "By-the-by, I received a record of Emerson's travels over the past six months."

She paused, eyeing me over the ripples of multicolored yarn cascading over her lap.

Drama does not take a holiday with the Belden-Tanner Agency.

Knowing I'd have to ask, I caved immediately. "Does it

coincide with the accidents?"

A sharp nod was the answer. "All but Vallejo and you've jolly well taken care of that, haven't you? I'm so relieved to see the pattern held. His office staff traveled with him. They were campaign stops."

Kevin flipped his silver dollar over his knuckles. "That puts both women in position."

Marcus smacked the board with the marker. "Can we check their money?"

"All four of them?" Mrs. C quivered in place. "A few calls should give us the big picture, eh?"

The puzzle for Redmond was complete. The two accidents and Emerson remained. I grimaced at the delineation my brain automatically made.

Marcus balanced his chin on his fists. Then he threw down his markers. "We need ice cream for brain fuel."

"Excellent idea." Mrs. C tossed aside her knitting and gathered herself to stand before I could draw breath. "You two stay there. The lads and I will get it set up."

I watched them walk into the kitchen. The bustle of bowls and spoons and ice cream options sounded on the air. I faced Kevin. "Wait. We had dessert at the restaurant."

Kevin put a finger on my lips. "They might hear you."

I chuckled, relieved at the break. I leaned my head against Kevin's arm which lay across the back of the sofa.

Studying the ceiling brought no answers. It did bring a call to the kitchen for a bowl of fudge ripple covered with walnuts and warm caramel sauce. So, it's hard to complain.

Kevin dipped a spoon into a vanilla and strawberry sauce combo. "The personal motives from Fleming and White's private lives don't work out."

"'s true." Mrs. C scooped up a dainty bite of hot fudge

and chocolate ice cream. "Only Redmond's was out of the pattern and he was the first to die."

I let the delicious mix of icy cold and warm flavors meld on my tongue. "The first one."

"Wait a minute." Marcus tapped a staccato rhythm on his bowl with his spoon. "You said family came first with the Feilens. They framed you for murder when you met TR."

Kevin shrugged. "I wasn't putting family first. I cost them millions. It was a test and I failed. You can't have everyone running their own game. It's all in or nothing."

The stark reality. There is only one ultimate loyalty. For the Feilens it's the con. Even at the cost of losing an asset like Kevin. Handsome. Articulate. Intelligent. Worth millions in a scam.

My hubby ate another bite of ice cream. He spoke without a trace of regret. "It all worked out. We're all family now."

A silent assent was aided by a circle of nods.

I licked caramel off my lip as I thought about what loyalty means to different people.

"All or nothing." I muttered the phrase. Suddenly, a new possibility lit up my mind. I licked off my spoon slowly. "All or nothing."

Marcus cocked his head to one side. "You said that already."

I shook my spoon at him. "What if Olsen hadn't appeared? If we take him out of the equation, what do we get?"

Mrs. C set her bowl on the side table, letting the spook rattle in it. "The first laddies were already dead. They died before he got there, didn't they?"

Marcus paused with ice cream at his mouth. "The

pattern was already in place. They disappeared on vacation."

Kevin sharpened, like a dog on point. "Vacation. Out of their routine. That phrase keeps popping. Someone made sure these deaths weren't connected."

"That was key." I settled my spoon in my empty bowl. "They couldn't be connected. Emerson saw the pattern, that's what made him dangerous."

Mrs. C made a half-hearted effort toward resuming her knitting. She grabbed the needles and pulled the yarn into her lap. However, she leaned forward, eyes gazing at me like a laser beam. "He wasn't an original target then, eh?"

I examined the theory. "I don't think so. I think in the last week or so, he said something to the wrong person. Or word got back to the wrong person."

Silence descended. I'd come this far. Where to next?

"The timeline." Marcus's yell could have woken the dead.

My heart jumped to my throat, racing wildly.

The boy jumped up, neatly avoiding his empty ice cream bowl. "Norton killing Redmond changes the timeline. We only have to worry about the other accidents. January and February."

While my child changed the whiteboard, I gathered the bowls. Kevin started to help, but I waved him back. "Filling a dishwasher is within my talents. Maybe I'll see a pattern."

Putting dishes inside the appliance didn't result in a new revelation. Studying Marcus's revised timeline did.

My gaze strayed to early fall, months before any known deaths. Green dollar signs marked August and September along with Richard Barsoom's name. Now the next date of interest wasn't until January.

"Long stretch." Rabi's low drawl pulled the words straight out of my brain.

I nodded slowly. "Mrs. C, be sure you get Barsoom's bank records for several months."

She sucked in a quick breath. A smile touched her lips. "Late summer, then?"

"Start there." I tapped my lip. Where to now?

Kevin clapped his hands. "I'm calling it. We have work and school tomorrow. We can't do anything else tonight."

Marcus groaned but it was half-hearted. Time eventually caught up with twelve-year-old boys. "I'm still sleeping at Mrs. C's to watch out for Rabi."

I exchanged a smile with Kevin. "That works for me."

Tuesday morning routine was... routine, including Marcus's warning not to solve the multiple murders during school hours.

When I told him it wasn't an issue, he turned on me.

"You can't be trusted. You get flashes of brilliance." He spoke in an accusing tone. Then he shook a finger at Kevin. "You, stop her."

Kevin scoffed. "That's what I'm here for. Tell me how."

The boy frowned in answer. He scowled at me in a final warning. "Three-fifteen."

I rolled my eyes at the boy and pointed behind him. "Go to school. Learn something useful."

§ § §

KEVIN and I spent the Tuesday morning meeting with the pale peach and burnt umber clients. They were thrilled. It had dried far better than I'd expected.

"You definitely earned your early bonus." Stanley, the slim, blond half of the partnership, toured the room, taking in the light from the open windows. "With the new paint, the foundation work, and the patio upgrades we can have it re-appraised. The increased value will give us leeway on the loan. That will give us operating capital."

More niceties followed while my brain tabulated our bonus. A nice little sum to put in our savings account. I'd had one before, but now there was money in the account.

I lagged behind while the three guys extolled the upgrades. Then, like a cop hammering for attention, a door burst open in my brain. Increased value. Timing. More cash.

I frowned as the words marched into my column for crossword clues. How did this relate to Emerson's death? The accidental deaths?

I stopped in my tracks. The voices faded into the distance.

Kevin appeared at the end of the hall. He spread out his hands in a question.

I waved him on. Let them sing his praises. He and the others had done the work. I slipped into a room done in soft teal. French doors looked out on the patio.

Hidden wealth. How to hide cash? Where did the money come from in the first place?

Did Barsoom or Phelps have hidden talents? Neither struck me as an original thinker. Someone else was in the scheme.

A quick call to Rabi and he was waiting when Kevin and I arrived at a local diner.

Mrs. C's text hit my phone at the same time.

We were seated in moments and ordered as soon as the waitress came. "The hot roast beef sandwich double mashed potatoes."

Once the waitress left, I wiggled my phone. "Mrs. C got a

confirmation on Phelps. An inheritance from a wealthy uncle. Straight out of a novel."

Kevin spun his glass of iced tea in the ring of condensation. "One less suspect."

I was as relieved as he sounded. "Rabi, what do you know about Barsoom's background?"

The other man didn't flinch at my abruptness. "Former army. Six years. Honorable discharge. Had some trouble."

"What trouble?" I asked.

Rabi's dark eyes met mine. "PTSD. Drugs. Turned it around."

A sad and all too common story for many veterans who returned from combat.

Kevin eyed me with a puzzled look. "What set you off this morning?"

"Hidden money." The phrase had forced its way into my crossword puzzle. "When whatshisname was talking about re-applying for the loan, it sparked something."

I spooned a forkful of potatoes and rich dark gravy into my mouth, groaning with delight.

The two men exchanged questioning glances.

"I'm not sure where it's going either, but it's in my puzzle and it won't leave." They were used to my crazy sounding chatter as if the crossword clues were living things with minds of their own. Which, they are.

"It's your subconscious talking." Kevin went with the more practical answer. "Go on."

"Motive has always been the question with selling the two accidents as murders." I paused to take a bite of Texas toast mixed with roast beast and gravy, getting my thoughts in order. "No one profits. So, why were they killed?"

I took another bite.

Kevin eyed me, waiting. "You don't know, yet."

I hurriedly swallowed. "Of course not. That's why I keep asking the question."

Rabi frowned at Kevin. "Should know that by now."

"Barsoom had gambling debts to the wrong people. Credit cards maxed out last year." I interjected, talking through the connected dots. "Now, your cousins say he's spending fast and loose. I'm betting he's got money in his savings account."

Kevin smiled. "Just like we do."

I gave him a teasing look. Financial ticks up the ladder clicked with my number skills. I jolted as another flash of lightning hit. I shook my fork at Kevin. "Shifting illegal cash. That's what your family does. Were you involved with that angle?"

The man gave me a flat stare from his gorgeous blue eyes. "What do you think?"

My hubby had been the frontline guy. "Stupid question. Fedor?"

Kevin's eyes narrowed. "Best of the three of us. Uncle Paulo was in charge of the accounts. Fedor can tell you most of the tricks."

I checked my puzzles again, but now they refused to talk to me. "I need Barsoom's background. I never did cross-check the names on those rosters against the VFW and Emerson's staff. I can do that now. There has to be a connection."

"You hope." Kevin pushed back his plate. "Jimbo's going to work with me getting ready for tomorrow's job. We need to pick up supplies to repair the pavilion at the park."

I licked off my fork, still trying to trace the tracks. "I'll be with you in spirit."

"Good to know." Kevin assured me with a smile. "Remember, don't solve the case without Marcus."

"Not in the next three hours I won't." My gaze shifted to Rabi. "Has Wilson called you?"

Rabi nodded. "We spoke."

No details. Wilson wanted a confession. No doubt he'd offered a deal, but he was pushing an immovable object.

Did the detective have enough to arrest Rabi without a confession? Thanks to a hesitant DA and Crawford's push to Wilson about bad publicity if he had to backtrack an arrest, Rabi was still on the streets. But the pressure was heating up from all sides.

I stacked my silverware on the plate. "They should have arrested you by now."

Rabi gave Kevin a silent nod. "You called it."

Kevin sipped his iced tea. "You're lucky she doesn't have a gold shield."

I tapped my lip. I brought up the names on the flight school and skydiving rosters. I scrolled through them slowly, absently thinking it was a shame I couldn't write this lunch off to a client.

Kevin looked around. "She hasn't brought our check. I have to go."

"My tab." Rabi answered without fanfare. "Business lunch for the case."

I laughed as he nodded to me, reading my mind. "I'm so obvious."

"One of the many reasons, I love you." Kevin stood, raising a hand of farewell to Rabi. Then he leaned over and brushed a kiss on my lips. "See you later. You and Rabi have to pick Marcus up."

"Will do," Rabi answered.

Part of me meant to respond, but my forebrain was studying names. "Richard Barsoom and Nick Phelps were at the airport the night Redmond was killed. Jocelyn Hopper and Helena Dayton were traveling with Emerson. Wait a minute. The pilot was Tim Dayton. He's got to be related to Helena."

"Her son." Rabi supplied.

I tapped my lip. "Did Emerson skydive? Lately, not in the military."

Rabi shook his head. He handed over his charge card to the waiter, then watched me silently.

My brain tabulated possible scenarios. "One of those three realized Norton killed Redmond that night. They saw how long it took for news of his disappearance to circulate and that no one suspected murder. But it was January before anyone else died."

Clues came and went. I considered possibilities.

"Who's the weakest link?" Time to get some answers. "Barsoom or Nick?"

"Barsoom." The answer was immediate. Rabi started to rise. "I can find him."

"We need…" *Barsoom alive*, were the words that popped into my head as I put a hand on Rabi's arm. "Evidence. The money trail. Let's see what Mrs. C found."

A SHORT TIME LATER, Rabi and I walked into Mrs. C's slice of Britain. From the Union Jack on her apartment window to a framed picture of her soccer team with the championship trophy from last year, her heritage was no longer hidden.

I smiled despite the seriousness of my and Rabi's visit. After fifty years hiding her identity, Mrs. C was free to be herself.

The older woman shuffled at top speed toward her kitchen table snuggled up next to the window facing the street. Her binoculars sat at the ready. Who needs a crime patrol when we have our one-woman watchdog at the ready?

"Not a social call, eh?" she asked as Rabi shut the door. "Not during business hours."

I pulled out a chair and sat down. "Have you gotten Barsoom's finances?"

Her eyes lit up as she pointed a blazing orange fingertip at me. "Just came through a bit ago. I've got the dirt on the ladies as well, Jocelyn and Helena. Haven't had the chance to take a look, have I? I printed it off. Can't focus on those computer screens."

"Neither can I," I admitted. "I'll make you a copy of Emerson's people."

In no time, we'd exchanged printouts. She had the two rosters. I had the financials. A quick showed nothing out of the ordinary on the two women's bank statements. Then, I studied Barsoom's.

"I'm glad you went back to last summer." They were dated through February. I put them side-by-side. "He was still paying over-charge fees and doing money transfers in July. Since the beginning of August, he's had a steady deposit every two weeks. That's a healthy payoff. His income from the VFW doesn't come close to accounting for it."

"Aye, he's in the chips now." The older woman's pale green eyes met mine. "And me friend can't track the source of the deposits."

"Can't?" Not won't. This woman and her ability to obtain information does not make me feel more secure. Honestly, there is no privacy anymore. I'm amazed at what I can find out as a PI.

Mrs. C tapped a finger on her lips. "They've an airport with a pilot involved, eh?"

I flipped through the bank statement. "Smuggling comes to mind, but I haven't heard of drug dealers who commit to regular wire transfers. This has to be..."

Words failed me.

"I don't have answers, but I bet Barsoom does." I eyed Rabi. "Will he talk to you?"

A stiff nod. "He'll talk."

If he knows what's good for him.

20

43 Down; 6 Letters;
Clue: A director's cue in filming
Answer: Action

R abi didn't waste time making calls. Without conversation, he drove a short distance and parked in a lot for Royal Gym. The place was a locally owned workout hub for up-and-coming yuppies. The only qualifications were too much money and the wish to see and be seen.

I'd never set foot inside any of their three convenient locations. Big surprise.

Could being a trainer at the gym be the source of his extra income? Why the secretiveness? Besides, no one paid personal trainers that much.

Rabi didn't go to the main entrance. He parked in the rear and walked to a backdoor.

Odd way to gain entry, but what did I know? "This doesn't seem to be your kind of gym."

A smile tipped up one side of his mouth. "Gentleman Joe's Boxing Ring."

"I remember that place." Joe's had hosted area boxing matches and trained local youths to keep them off the streets for decades. Shortly after I arrived in Langsdale, Joe's, along with a number of the old-time businesses, closed. The resort side of the city priced out the neighborhood places.

Rabi walked up to a metal door. He gripped the door latch and depressed the lever. Setting his legs, he braced his left hand against the frame. Then he jerked upward with a hard wrench.

The door opened without a sound.

"Known flaw." Rabi explained as he gestured for me to enter. "Joe never fixed the lock."

"Do tell." I walked into a deserted corridor. It looked to run the length of the building.

The clatter of weights hitting the floor mixed with yells and raised voices of encouragement. The smell was a pungent mix of cleansers coupled with sweat.

A number of doors opened onto the hall from the left.

I'd gone roughly halfway down, when a tall, athletic white woman with bobbed hair stepped in front of me.

She pulled back instantly.

"I didn't see you." She did a double-take at Rabi, then checked the corridor behind us.

"My associate and I are here to see the manager." I pivoted from the plan of finding Barsoom for a more direct line to the money trail. "Would you direct me?"

The women's scowl deepened. She took a deep breath.

"Brook, who are you talking to? Your new client is waiting." A well-muscled young man stepped into the doorway. His eyes widened as he took in Rabi and me.

"Thank you. I'll take it from here." I dismissed Brook with a polite smile and stern look, waiting until she conceded and walked away.

It's amazing how far attitude will take you.

I squared off with the guy and repeated the line about speaking with the manager. Keep your opponent off balance and take control of the situation. Those two rules have served well over the years.

The new guy, also doing a double-take at Rabi standing silently behind me, checked out the corridor behind us.

I flipped over his nametag. "Paul, is your manager on-site?"

He straightened his shoulders, which still kept him at eye level with me. His mouth tightened to a straight line, evidently annoyed that he couldn't use his height to look down on me. "The manager isn't in today. Can I help you?"

"Are you the assistant manager?" I asked. "If not, lead me to the next in command."

I was tired of his power plays. Was it my fault no one else walked in via the locked back door?

Paul threw his hands up in surrender. "Tim's up front. Follow me."

Tim? As in Dayton, the pilot? What were the odds?

As we walked Rabi was at my side. I let the distance to Paul increase. "Would the pilot know you?"

Rabi shook his head.

No doubt he didn't need to see beginners sky dive. Reassured, I caught up with Paul as he turned the corner. A glass wall on the right gave a view of the full gym. Stationary bikes. Treadmills. Weight machines. Individual stations.

The space reminded me of a football game on a snowy day. A few diehards but they weren't enough to pay the rent.

A cluster of four guys in the front corner caught my attention. Barsoom. He was looking away fortunately. I didn't recognize the other three.

Rabi saw him as well. His gaze studied the other three. He gave a short nod.

I assumed he knew at least one of the other men.

Paul led the way into a small office, past two other trainer types. He knocked on a closed door. "Tim? Someone wants to see you."

After a grunt from inside, he let himself in.

I searched and found the name plate on the desk. Timothy Dayton, the pilot. The spiderweb was growing by the hour.

Dayton swiveled his chair away from a desktop display. His jaw tightened as he caught sight of us.

I had a brief glimpse sight of a spreadsheet. My eyes tracked the headings. Admission date. OR. Diagnoses. Supplies. That was all I got before he locked the screen.

He stood, scowling at all three of us. "What are you doing bringing them here? Do you wish to sign up for a membership?"

"They were in the back hall." Paul spoke as if Tim were to blame. "They insisted on seeing someone in management."

From the exchange of angry glares and the petulant tones, Tim and Paul were not exercise buddies.

Rabi stood to one side, placing a hand on the door. His attitude made it clear it was time for Paul to leave.

The trainer smirked as he walked out, evidently happy to throw this problem to Tim.

The pilot pasted on a neutral expression. "And you are?"

"Tracy Belden." I held out my hand, still working on my next line. It's always an interesting choice between admitting I'm a PI or feeding them a line. Introducing Rabi as my associate made me feel like I was either with the mob or the FBI. It was a thin line.

"I'm investigating a series of murders." I left the ominous word hanging in the air, relishing the shock on Dayton's face. "The trail has led me to a number of your employees."

One guy who may or may not be on the books. Okay, a slight exaggeration.

I gestured to his chair. "Why don't you sit?"

He was halfway down before it struck him that it was his office.

I settled myself in a padded chair and waited for him to do the same.

Rabi folded his arms and leaned against the door, per his usual.

Dayton started to talk to Rabi, checked himself, and faced me. "Who are working for? You're not a cop."

Since Rabi had paid Marcus five dollars, the Belden Tanner Agency had an official client. "I'm a private investigator. My client list is confidential."

And standing three feet to my left.

Dayton's shoulders relaxed. He leaned back in his swivel chair. "I don't have to talk to you."

I gave him my best smile. "No, you don't. I can go to the police with what I know."

He straightened a notebook on his desk. "Just out of curiosity, what murders are you talking about?"

Best to start at the beginning of a long list. "For one, Miles Redmond."

His frown and relief were instantaneous and almost comical. "Who?"

If this guy was the mastermind, the criminals wouldn't have made it as far as they did. He evidently had never been told the first victim's name. Or he truly was ignorant.

"Last November." I sat back and launched into the story. The affair. The confrontation. The dead body. I watched the man closely. "There was a class for beginner pilots at the airport."

His expression stilled.

I continued with my second jab. "Another for sky diving. You flew the plane."

The tightness around his eyes relaxed. Why?

He held my gaze with a rigid control, as if forcing himself not to blink or look away.

I'd missed something. What? When I mentioned him flying the plane? Where else would a pilot be?

Perhaps teaching new pilots would put him on the ground, closer to the action. Why was he relieved to be next to a murder rather than in the air?

"You'll have to forgive me. I can't help." He shifted forward. His relief was patent. "It's hard to see anything from ten miles away and ten thousand feet up."

"I'm sure you have a great deal of information to offer." I assured him. "You know everyone involved."

He frowned. "You said the guy confessed. What do you need from me? Besides, that's only one murder. You spoke of several deaths."

I scooted forward on the chair, waiting, watching. Being annoying. I like to go with my strong suit. "The others are more recent. One man died in January."

A complete freeze followed by a quick recovery. He was getting his feet underneath him.

He pasted on a concerned expression. "Are you saying

they were related to our exercise programs? Were they clients here?"

An interesting opening. "That's what I'd like to confirm. Could you give me a list of your members?"

"Absolutely not." He drew back, closing the door on that front. "Tell me their names and I'll check."

I rarely win at poker, but I knew enough not to show my hand. I rattled off the names of four of my more annoying high-school classmates. Not surprisingly, none of them were enrolled at the gym.

As far as I knew, they weren't dead either.

Pushing the computer monitor to one side, Tim put his arms on his desk and faced me directly. He could afford to take charge now that I'd strayed away from his past. "What led you to us?"

I gave him back an innocent, trusting expression. "A tip. The people involved mentioned in-depth workouts with a personal trainer. They weren't sure of the specific gym the victims attended."

His lip rose to a sneer. "From what you've said, these deaths hardly constitute murder. If it did, the police would be involved. Not some second rate, soccer mom, beginner PI."

Rude. "Don't knock soccer moms."

Tim pointed to the door. "If the police need any information, they can contact us. Otherwise, this interview is over. Please leave."

I stood and pivoted toward the door. His whole body melted with relief, that's when I spun on my heel.

Tim had stepped around the desk. This put us nose to nose.

Once I shifted forward, he was forced to retreat.

His jaw tightened. Annoyance filled his eyes.

Better people than him had failed to get rid of me so easily. "Do you know Richard Barsoom?"

He had no time to hide the flash of recognition at Barsoom's name.

I pushed on. "Is he one of your trainers?"

Tim drew in a breath, taking time to frame the answer. "He's assisted us a few times in the past. He is not on staff on a permanent basis."

"And not certified, I bet." I underlined the accusation in my tone.

Tim smirked. "He's never worked as a trainer."

I frowned, noting the triumph in his voice. "Then what does he do?"

"I told you." Tim slowly drew in a breath.

Buying time? Striving for control? Planning to push me bodily out of the office? After he glanced at Rabi, I was betting on the latter option.

After weighing his chances, the man regained control. "Richard has assisted us in setting up stations and in giving demonstrations. That's all I can tell. You'll have to excuse me. I have a meeting."

"Of course." I was completely agreeable, so accommodating. "Is Richard here today, by chance?"

A frown, pausing for time. Tell the truth or lie? What would get rid of me sooner. "I think I saw him earlier. I couldn't say."

I pointed toward where I thought the main part of the gyn stood. "Do you mind if we go look?"

"Sure," Tim spoke through gritted teeth. "Sign in at the front desk for a visitor's tag."

"Absolutely." I waved an assurance as I headed for the door.

A moment later, Rabi and I had worked our way to the

not so secure back door. I raised a brow at the warning that alarms would sound if opened.

Rabi repeated the braced feet, lifting the door upward maneuver that had gotten us inside. No alarm sounded.

A moment later, we stood in the sun. We started walking to the side of the building.

Rabi wordlessly pointed at a shiny black Corvette.

"Richard's car. Nice." I admired the bartender's taste, if not his apparent lack of morals. "How long do you think it'll take him? You want to set the over under at five minutes?"

Rabi raised a brow.

"Okay," I surrendered in the face of the man's noncommittal response. I took out my phone and set a timer. "To make it sporting let's go for two minutes, thirty seconds. Any longer and I'll buy the iced mochas."

I figured Tim would be nervous enough to light a fire under Richard. After all, the bartender couldn't fail to recognize Rabi's description. There are few souls on the planet who relish facing Rabi, especially if you've been picking off his friends over the last few months.

The back door opened with nine seconds left.

I held my breath, waiting to see the person's face. With my luck, it would be the janitor emptying trash.

I fisted a hand in the air at the sight of the well-muscled bartender bolting for his car. "Yes."

Rabi spared a nod as I held out my phone as proof.

Barsoom was too busy looking over his shoulder at the inside hall to notice us. Then he was running to the car while pulling his keys out of his pocket.

A few strides put Rabi directly behind the other man.

A deliberate scuff on the concrete froze Barsoom in place.

He was practically shaking as he looked over his shoulder. Facing Rabi's stern expression sent a spasm through the bartender's body. His hand jerked, dropping the keyring to the ground.

Rabi moved left.

Barsoom matched the move, leaving him with his back against his car. With no room for retreat or escape. Just as I liked it.

---

21

50 Across; 6 Letters;
Clue: A trip taken for pleasure
Answer: Outing

I bent over and retrieved the keys, tossing them up and down in my hand. "I think it's time we all had a little talk, Richard."

Fifteen minutes later, Rabi, Richard, and I were sitting at an out of the way park. Almost deserted at this time of day, but the snack bar was open for limited service.

I'd called Kevin on the drive over. "Are you at a stopping place? I got a little carried away and Rabi and I can't pick up Marcus. We're about to have a discussion with Barsoom about his recent activities."

"I'll get Marcus," Kevin agreed without hesitation. "Hold on the interrogation until we get there. I'm not taking this hit for you."

"Fine. We'll wait until you and the boy child arrive." I

met Rabi's gaze in the rearview mirror. I couldn't stop a smile.

Rabi's eyes lit up with laughter.

I gave Kevin the name of the park where we were headed. "You might as well stop and pick up Mrs. C, too. Or I'll never hear the end of how no one tells her anything."

With her spy network, why do I need to keep her informed?

After I hung up, silence descended.

Barsoom hadn't spoken a word. He cast nervous glances at Rabi then at the landscape outside the car. He looked to be weighing his chances of escape.

"Relax." A criminal should have more control. "Your nerves are getting on my nerves."

He jerked around to look at me. "I don't have to talk to you."

People have been saying that to me all week. "You agreed to come."

Barsoom never had a chance. Rabi would have intimidated a stone gargoyle.

When we pulled into the park, Kevin, Marcus, and Mrs. C were sitting at a corner table on the outside patio.

I shut the door and urged a reluctant Barsoom to start walking. Rabi joined us at the front of the car.

The bartender gestured toward the trio. "You brought your child to an interrogation? What kind of mother are you?"

"Don't worry about my parenting." I had to bite back a laugh. Little did he know that my past cases had included breaking and entering, hotwiring cars, and an episode involving stolen lizards. "We're just going to have a friendly chat. The three of us."

Barsoom glared at me. "You can't kill me in front of witnesses."

Kevin snorted.

I burst out laughing. "If you think they'll protect you, you've misread the dynamics of this group. I'm the nice one."

Marcus rolled his eyes. With lemonade and French fries to his right and his phone on his left, the boy was ready. "No, she's not. She's mean."

Mrs. C had hot tea and a plateful of small muffins.

The peanut gallery was set. Movie nights. Game nights. Interrogations. I felt like I was at the old Roman circus where criminals were killed for the amusement of the masses.

When Barsoom headed for their table, Rabi took his arm and directed him to one close by.

I enforced the decision from his other side. "You're not getting within arm's length of my son. If you try anything at all, this won't end well for you."

I sat facing Barsoom. Rabi was on my left, facing Marcus and the others at the next table.

Barsoom shot a nervous glance at Rabi and took a deep breath as an apparent effort to gather his remaining nerve. "You have no right --"

"Button it." I raised a hand to stop his protests. "I'm also not going to listen to your alleged innocence. If you aren't guilty, why did you bolt when Tim told you we were looking for you?"

Barsoom sneered. "My training session was over. I was leaving."

"We'll do this my way." I swept away his excuse. "I have your bank account statements for the last several months."

The man slapped the table. "How dare you? How did you get my personal information?"

"I'm a detective." I raised my voice while doing a happy dance inside. My boss, Crawford, throws that phrase in my face every chance he gets. I love doing the same to other people. Crawford is right. It's fun. "Any supposed invasion of privacy is the least of your worries."

The man's wide-eyed surprise as an expression of false innocence was good but pointless.

"You've been living large for most of a year." I stabbed the table. "Not from bartending or gym training. The funds aren't traceable to any legitimate business."

That wasn't technically true. We hadn't progressed that far. We didn't have the resources. Crawford's office was working on the trail.

Barsoom's Adam's apple bobbed up and down as he swallowed hard. "I do consulting work."

"For what?" I scoffed. "Mixing martinis? You pulled in enough to pay off all your gambling and credit card debts. A new car. Trips to Vegas."

At the mention of Vegas, the guy jerked as if I'd struck him. "Those were my private affairs. Not... um... nothing."

The reaction was out of all proportion to my words. I'd only thrown in the Vegas reference since Marcus mentioned the travel in relation to the expensive life style.

Note to self – taking wild shots works. I've always been glad my subconscious knows where to strike. Most of the time, I don't. Although...

My peripheral vision caught my son typing madly away on his phone.

I searched my memory for the name of the person who'd died in Vegas and when. Marcus mentioned Barsoom had gone visiting recently.

My phone vibrated. Holding Barsoom's gaze as long as I could, I swiped my thumb on the screen. The text was from Marcus.

"Tahoe in January, Fleming. Vegas in Feb. Same as Kyle White's death."

I set the phone down in a slow, deliberate gesture. My nails tapped the back like a death knell. "You've been a busy boy, Richard. This is not good news for you. Even worse, I now have solid leads the police can track. Dates. Places. They love evidence."

The bartender's breath came fast and ragged. His gaze flipped from the phone to me. "You don't have anything."

"I have your travel dates to Vegas that coincide with Kyle White's death while rock climbing." I let the facts sink in. "An odd way to die for a longtime mountain climber."

Barsoom shook his head, his shoulders had lost their stiffness. "He was getting up in years. Accidents--"

I continued as if he hadn't spoken. "I also have your trip to Tahoe in January, when Fleming had an accident. That's a lot of coincidences, even for me. For the police, that is way over the top."

"What? No." The man honestly looked puzzled. He met Rabi's hard gaze without flinching, still befuddled. "Those were working trips with my girlfriend."

"And who would that be?" I shot out the question.

"Jocelyn Hopper." He answered without hesitation.

Of course, Emerson's executive assistant and his office manager had both been at the scene of the accidents.

The connection didn't prove either of them were involved.

Too bad I still didn't have a clue what the excess money or the deaths were about. Not that I could reveal how little I knew.

The breeze carried a murmur of voices, including the lilt of a British accent. Checking on Jocelyn perhaps? With so many the players on-board, we hadn't had time for a thorough background check on all of them.

I had work. Marcus had school and Mrs. C had afternoon soccer matches to watch. We were spread thin.

However, Kevin would be the first to tell anyone about my gift for spinning theories out of a few facts and a lot of make believe. I also had a nervous, weak-willed criminal in front of me.

"Richard." I lowered my voice to a friendly level and reached for his hands.

He pulled them off the table and drew back from me.

Again, I just kept talking. "Once the police exhume the bodies, they'll find evidence of foul play. Bruises in the wrong places, such as on the arms or the back, will still show up."

"No, I... It was..." Barsoom stumbled into silence. His hand shook as he wiped the sweat off his upper lip.

I waited a beat before speaking. "No one was supposed to get hurt? A victimless crime?"

I pictured Tim's spreadsheet with the medical entries. Throw in the VFW, sky diving, and the gyms. Was this money due to false claims?

My phone buzzed. A glance showed the trio at the next table had reached the same conclusion. Insurance fraud.

Barsoom was still sputtering like a broken record.

I flashed the phone's message to Rabi. His nod was one of indifference. "You did all of this to collect insurance payments? Medical fraud? How much money could there be in that?"

"Oh, luv, buckets and buckets." Mrs. C's comment floated over with a note of admonishment.

"Yeah," Marcus chimed in as well. "This is a ton of money. Millions, I bet."

Blame the logical portion of my brain, but I was still trying to figure out the profit margin. "Do you have the patients involved in this? Are they actually injured?"

"No need." Kevin's confident tone couldn't have carried beyond our two tables. "They have a man at a computer, an MD's license to file under, and access to names and insurance information. No one is ever seen. The tests are never done. Pure profit. Drugs, operations. Billed for but never done."

A non-judgmental tone colored his comment.

"Hey!" Barsoom half rose out of his chair. He pointed at them. "They can't help."

I choked back a laugh. "What do you think this is? A game? If I don't get the right answers, you go home?"

Rabi grabbed the other man and pulled him down.

Barsoom's outrage melted. His shocked gaze and drooping mouth were almost comical. The realization was evidently just hitting him that his former life was over. He buried his head in his hands, as if his spine couldn't hold up the weight any longer.

"It's over." I have to admit at this point, I rolled my eyes at his defeated frame. I was out of patience with his stupidity.

Why do criminals never see themselves getting caught? No escape plan. No take the money and run. But when is there ever enough money to satisfy greed?

I glanced at Kevin, thinking of his family, Fedor and Safina, who might be planning on leaving town with ill-gotten gains.

"Sit up." Returning my focus to Barsoom, I smacked the

table, hard. "What you do now is going to determine how much time you serve in jail."

The bartender straightened as if he'd been tased. "Jail? As in the penitentiary?"

"He's clueless." Marcus's judgment carried in the thin air.

"Poor lad's proper gutted, he is." Mrs. C was less condemning. "Definitely not the brains, eh?"

"Fraud. Murder. They're felonies. That's hard time." My hand made a chopping motion on the table. "The paths and timing all lead to you."

Barsoom raked a hand through his hair. "I didn't kill anybody. I didn't even know their deaths were connected. I thought they were accidents when I heard about them."

Denial. Self-delusion. It's a great skill to have for the weak willed.

"Why were these people targeted?" My voice rose in frustration. I leaned forward, until Rabi raised a hand and gently pushed my back.

Always on alert, the man took no chances.

I nodded my thanks. "Richard. When were White and Fleming together at the VFW? Over New Year's, a post-holiday poker game, perhaps?"

I continued with my guesses. "They stayed in the back room after closing time. You were cleaning up. Someone came in."

"Tim." Barsoom's gaze zeroed in on a spot on the table. "I gave him a beer. I forgot anyone else was in the place. At first, he was talking about the money he'd won on his football bets."

He stopped, probably wishing like so many others, that he could jump back to the fateful moment that had destroyed a future.

"We were never to discuss the operation in public." Barsoom raised his gaze. "He thought we were alone. He started crowing about the easy money and expanding the operation. He mentioned one of the regulars we'd used for an ortho procedure. White came out of the back hall, with an empty pitcher in his hand. Bad luck."

"Karma," came Marcus's stage whisper. "It'll get ya."

I cocked my head to one side. "He asked about this nonexistent injury to someone he knew hadn't been hurt?"

Barsoom nodded. "My heart stopped in my chest. Tim went white. I told him we were talking about someone at the gym. Similar name. I said to forget about it."

Rabi had followed every revelation with stoic silence. "The man was an MP. A talker. Tenacious."

The former bartender, soon to be prisoner, confirmed the judgement with a sigh. "Tim and I heard him tell Fleming. Even then, I thought it was no problem. What could they do? Ask the guy? He'd deny it. Done deal."

"But Tim told her, didn't he?" I could see Tim wanting to cover his lapse as if I'd been at his elbow. Was it Jocelyn or Helena or both? I couldn't let on that I still didn't know.

"Tim told Jocelyn the next week." Barsoom was still eyeing the table.

I rapped the table where the man was staring until he looked me. "Were she and Tim the only other ones involved?"

He nodded. No Helena.

I continued putting the next scenes in place. "Since she was behind the fraud and she took the biggest cut of the pie, she had the most to lose."

Barsoom paused while rubbing his face. "We were all equal."

"Sure, you were."

I don't know who in the peanut gallery spoke, but from the muffled laughter, the watchers had few illusions about the honor of thieves.

I was stunned at his naivete. I studied my short, chipped nails, gathered my wits, then tried to shatter the block of ice sitting opposite me.

When my phone rang, it was almost a relief. I glanced at Marcus. All three of them held up empty hands. The readout said Crawford, my bossman, who actually owns the detective agency and employees me as a PI. "What's up?"

"An arrest warrant's been issued." His voice, usually the volume of a megaphone, was a bare whisper for him.

I didn't have to take my phone away from my ear. I kept my gaze on Richard to keep up the connection and the pressure.

Rabi whose instincts had kept him alive for countless missions wasn't fooled. "The warrant is live."

Crawford's old office chair squeaked over the phone line. "It would be better if he gave himself up."

I had to cover my mouth from laughing out loud. "Don't worry. We'll be headed down to the station soon. Tell Wilson we're bringing a surprise visitor."

Without a fare thee well, I hung up on my bossman. Let him stew.

"Richard," I spoke slowly and softly. "The two people who were at the VFW the night you spoke with Tim are dead. You were present at the time and location of those deaths."

He started shaking his head halfway through my statement.

I reached over and put my hand on his arm. "Denial and pleas of ignorance aren't going to cut it when you get to court."

His eyes widened like a deer who'd just heard the gunshot. He stared at me then his mouth, literally, fell open.

"Someone is going to pay for those murders." I spaced out the words, hammering them home like nails in a coffin. No reaction. Nothing. Nobody was home. "When did you realize they were being targeted?"

Perhaps a direct question would work better, because his brain appeared to be frozen.

Barsoom swallowed hard. "Weeks ago. I mean, people come and go. They get busy. They got sick. They stop coming in."

The out-of-town locations. The time between the deaths. "The murders were well planned."

Richard buried his head in his hand. "Maria, the waitress, mentioned it had been a bad year for our regulars. She rattled off several names. When I heard those two, I knew."

I rapped the table with my knuckles. "Did you sabotage Fleming's brakes? Or push White off the cliff?"

I didn't believe the bartender had the brains to plan the deaths or the nerve to carry out the deed.

His head shot up. He held out his hands first to me, then he looked at Rabi. "I would never."

Rabi's stern expression could have been carved from granite. He shifted forward a bare inch. "Who?"

Richard held the dark gaze for an endless minute. "They were business trips. She had to accompany Emerson."

His voice gradually drifted lower and lower until I had to strain to hear the words.

"It was Jocelyn." His lips barely moved. "She did it. She killed them."

---

22

51 Across; 6 Letters;
Clue: Furtive; Sly
Answer: Sneaky

Marcus likes to think of the Langsdale Police station as his home away from home. Several of his school essays centered around the behind-the-scenes happenings and the men and women who work there with no public recognition.

After the first few papers, his teachers think I'm a cop. Once I explain I'm a PI they're pretty understanding. For good or ill, one of my son's skills is his ability to flash a smile and wiggle his way under the strongest defenses.

So, of course, all five members of the Belden Tanner Agency accompanied Richard to the police department. Rabi was being questioned. This time as a witness, not a suspect.

Richard was being given the third degree.

I walked into the waiting room, after having a friendly, voices raised discussion with Wilson about holding out on him, misleading suspects, and the usual outrage.

Marcus met me at the waiting room door when I entered. "We heard what you guys said. Wilson was mad."

"A little." I joined Kevin, who'd been staring out the window at the dying day.

My hubby put his arm around my waist. "Wilson gets credit for solving four murders."

Mrs. C smiled over the knitting needs. "And putting a stop to the medical fraud."

I leaned against Kevin, welcoming his solid strength and warmth. "They have Tim in custody. They confiscated his work and home computers. If he was smart, he should have deleted the files after we left. He had to know we were on to him. Although, I didn't know the details at that time."

Kevin snorted, covering a laugh. "You're not nearly greedy enough to be a good criminal."

My son nodded. "No amount of money is enough. You're too smart, too. Most people don't know when to stop."

"Thank you." I bowed to Marcus. "Wilson put out a BOLO for Jocelyn Hopper. The Carson City police have been alerted to look for her. They'll take her computers as well. Work and home. Once they download the GPS records on the phones, it should give them the evidence they need to put them at the scene of the deaths."

"The victims knew her from the VFW and the skydiving get-togethers." Kevin's voice was analytical. "A woman approached them. A friendly wave. Neither man would have been on their guard. I'm betting White was dead before the car went over the cliff."

Rabi stared across the room. The scenes were easy to

imagine. "Leverage, not strength. Catch your opponent unaware. A push. Done."

I took a deep breath glad the bizarre case was almost over. "Emerson was right. They were targeted. He just never knew why."

"What about the other lady, Helena?" Marcus asked.

I'd been wrong about her. "Richard swears Helena Dayton isn't involved. Jocelyn and Tim put the pieces together three years ago when they met at the VFW. She used to work in a hospital and he had experience with an insurance company. Turns out Richard is Tim's cousin. Tim got drunk last summer and bragged about the money. Richard was drowning in debt and insisted on a cut. He helped with the paperwork on the fake accidents."

Mrs. C sighed in disgust, multiplying the wrinkles on her fact. "He's the bloody weak link."

Marcus threw back his shoulders and crossed his arms over his chest. "Is Rabi in the clear?"

"Technically, yes." I'd won, yet I hadn't crossed the finish line. "Officially, they haven't removed him as a suspect."

Anger darkened Marcus's expression.

Rabi put a hand on the boy's shoulder. "I'm good."

I also held out a hand to forestall my son's outburst. "The arrest warrant is on hold. Wilson believes Jocelyn is the killer, but the DA's under pressure. He needs someone on record for the murder of a state senator."

Kevin's phone rang as I spoke, Fedor, he mouthed silently.

His greeting was in code. They used it to confirm they were talking to the correct person and no one was under duress.

The Feilens leave *nothing* to chance.

Kevin listened silently for a few seconds. "Rabi's not clear."

I thought a heard a snatch of "—she doing?"

"My best." I yelled at the phone. "You get over here and solve it."

"I'll tell Tracy you have the utmost confidence in her ability." Kevin laughed and pocketed his phone before taking my hand. He pulled me toward the door. "Let's head home."

Mrs. C picked up her bag. "It's going to be dinner soon, eh? Let's find a nice pub on the way. I'll stand for the finger food."

Rabi held out his hand to help her to her feet. "I got the meal. Finish my tab with the agency."

"Those are the two best offers I've had all day." I was more than ready to quit the police station. "Jocelyn will turn up. Wilson will get the truth, and the DA will get the murderer."

Marcus planted himself in front of us, holding out both his hands to stop us. "I'm staying with Mrs. C again."

Kevin turned the boy child around to face the door and walked him into the hall with us. "You are going to have to live with Tracy and me eventually."

"Tomorrow," Marcus promised. "But I was promised a vacation."

"So was I." I squeezed Kevin's hand, happy to have one more night alone with my hubby.

The elevator dinged when our family group was several feet away.

I happened to be closest. When the door opened, I automatically stopped and put my arm out to block Marcus. At a police station there's no telling who might come out.

Jocelyn Hopper saw me at the same instant I recognized

her. Her jaw tightened. "What is she doing here? Are you responsible for spreading these lies about me? I've done nothing."

"Oh, please." I'd had a long weekend. I didn't need her to add to it. "Tell Wilson your troubles. Then he can tell you that Richard Barsoom already flipped on you. By now, the police have your computers. By the way, you were a little sloppy on Fleming's death."

Anger sparked in her eyes. "What are you saying? If White and Fleming were killed, Richard did it. He must have murdered Senator Emerson, too. I told Richard that Emerson was going to botanical gardens to confront the reporter. Richard was petrified they'd uncovered his medical insurance fraud."

"Blaming Richard for the murders won't work." I advanced on the woman. "You, he, and Helena were all in the vicinity when White and Fleming were killed. But Helena was with the caterer all afternoon when Fleming fell off the cliff. Richard was in the hotel spa."

Jocelyn gritted her teeth. "I told him..."

I raised my brows. "Told him to stay out of sight? Spiked his drink with sleeping pills, perchance? He told Wilson. He said he felt sleepy but went for a massage. Did you forget that he's a big boy with a tolerance for drugs thanks to his PTSD? That means he couldn't have pushed White off the cliff."

The other woman's face stilled. Her narrowed gaze studied me, evidently in the hopes I was lying.

"All true." I met her gaze head on. I have to admit, I was getting into this showdown. "Barsoom didn't follow Emerson to the gardens. He claims he was at the gym. The police will find witnesses to confirm his story. You followed

Emerson. I'm betting the police will find witnesses to put you at the location of each murder."

The office manager shook her head. "Helena and Tim _-"

"Stop!" I may have stomped my foot at this point. "Olsen was digging into the rumors of corruption in Emerson's campaign. You thought he'd stumbled onto your fraud. *You* followed Emerson to my wedding. You saw him argue with Rabi then Olsen. When they both left, you confronted him."

Jocelyn fisted her hands, but there was no escaping the truth.

I cocked my head to one side. "What did you think when you realized, Olsen had spoken to Emerson about his war record? I'll bet you'd already blurted out an excuse about the fraud. Did you confess to a crime your boss knew nothing about?"

A harsh breath escaped through Jocelyn's gritted teeth. "You are as annoying as everyone said you were."

"It's a gift." Marcus's voice floated up from behind me.

"It's true." I never took my eyes off the other woman. "Once you mentioned your crime, you couldn't let Emerson walk away. He was a big man. A touch arrogant. Sure of himself. He never thought you'd strike him down from behind. That's the only way it could have happened. He fell in the water and you held him under."

She drew herself up straight. "There's no proof."

"Someone will have seen you." I scoffed in her face. "Security cameras have multiplied like rabbits. One of them will show you in the wrong place at the wrong time. You were the one who shot at Olsen and trashed him room looking for his notes. Someone will have seen you there."

"Get me out of here." Jocelyn tossed her head. She shot a

look at the officers at her sides. "I don't have to listen to her. She's not the police."

Wilson stepped forward wearing a polite expression. "I've been telling people that all weekend. Take Ms. Hopper to interrogation room one."

After she walked away, Wilson looked at me, then at Rabi. "I spoke with the DA. He's canceled the arrest warrant for you. All charges are dropped."

Rabi nodded. "Thank you."

Then Wilson turned to eye Kevin and me. "Congratulations to both of you on your wedding. Now, please--."

"Wait! You can't leave." Olsen's voice was accompanied by the sound of running footsteps.

I groaned aloud and cast a pleading look at Wilson. "Can you shoot him? Or at least keep him locked up?"

Wilson looked sympathetic, but he shook his head. "I wish."

Olsen skidded to a stop in front of Rabi. "Mr. Rabi, I need five minutes of your time. Now that Senator Emerson is dead the truth can come out. I'm writing a story that will reveal the circumstances about the medal he earned under fraudulent conditions."

Rabi stared down at the reporter. "No, you're not."

The other man stood there with his mouth flapping open. It took a full minute for him to draw breath and try again. "You can't --"

Rabi leaned forward. He looked like a vulture hanging over his victim. "He blew the bridge. Saved the village. I was the superior officer. I ordered him to leave. No lies."

"I have a report." Olsen stepped back and swallowed hard. "I can write the story."

Rabi snapped his fingers.

The echo reverberated through the hall like a gunshot.

Several people, including me jumped.

The tall silent man pointed at Olsen. "Emerson was a friend. Don't call him a liar. Or me."

He stepped toward Olsen, coming within inches of the other man who quickly retreated. Rabi walked on by and stepped into the open elevator.

The reporter's outrage quickly returned. He met my gaze. "He can't stop the press."

Kevin stepped between us. "Jack Rabi is a war hero. He has more medals and missions than Emerson could ever claim. He also has more contacts than you do. He also knows someone who knows your father."

My husband spoke in a straightforward, factual oh-so-reasonable tone.

The fighting tension left Olsen's shoulders. He gestured toward the elevator as he opened his mouth.

Kevin stopped him. "You have your story. War hero tragically cut down while trying to unmask fraud. It's great. It's popular. Take the win."

Comforting. Encouraging. Was I the only one who heard the touch of steel in his tone?

I joined Kevin in the elevator.

Deep furrows marked Olsen's brow. His gaze went from Rabi's deadly stare to Kevin's encouraging expression. Finally, the reporter's whole body deflated. "Fine. I can make that work."

I wiggled my finger in farewell.

When the elevator closed, Kevin pulled me into his arms.

I threw my arms around his neck.

"Are you two going to be kissing all the time?" Marcus asked.

Kevin and I looked at him together. "Yes."

23

1 Across; 8 Letters;
Clue: A favorable action
Answer: Good deed

I 'll skip to Wednesday morning. Honestly, after confronting Barsoom then Jocelyn then Olsen, I felt like a worn-out dishrag.

Marcus stayed home from school. Not that I wasn't ready for a good debate, but it didn't seem fair for the boy to miss the wrap-up. He and Kevin made blueberry pancakes, bacon, eggs, the whole bit.

I love guys who can cook.

Rabi and Mrs. C arrived within minutes of each other.

When Marcus opened his mouth, I held up my hand. "We're not discussing the case while I eat. My brain needs a break."

"That's not what I was going to say." The boy child spoke

in a self-righteous tone. "I was about to ask Kevin if my new aunt and cousin were going to join us today."

Kevin saluted Marcus for the quick recovery as he passed around the serving platter of pancakes. "They left last night on the red-eye for Paris."

"That was sudden." I did a doubletake. "I thought they'd stop to say good-bye and get the low down on the case."

"I didn't expect them to hang around." Kevin met my gaze. He showed no surprise at his relatives' quick departure.

Mrs. C looked up from dousing her scrambled eggs with a goodly helping of hot sauce. "They seemed very interested in the case. Called again at the pub to ask if Rabi was off the hook."

Marcus grinned. "They were *thrilled* to hear Jocelyn was officially in custody."

I took a bite of crispy bacon, relishing the salty taste as it melted in my mouth. "Something about this doesn't sound right."

Kevin pointed his fork at my plate. "Eat your breakfast. We're not supposed to discuss the case."

Happy to oblige, I focused on the delicious meal. For the first time in days, I could relax.

We were finishing up breakfast when Crawford called my cell phone.

"Are your new in-laws still in town?" He didn't even bother to say hello.

I frowned at the phone. "Good morning to you, too. Why are you calling again? I've already talked to you once today, and my in-laws left last night."

I cast a questioning look at my hubby.

"That didn't take long." Kevin reached for the remote for the small television on the kitchen counter.

"Turn on the news." Was Crawford's only response.

"Breaking News." The well-known face of a popular Asian female announcer filled the screen. "California real-estate moguls, Theodore and Nina Kelsey were robbed of six million dollars of bearer bonds late, last night."

I gasped, both at the huge amount and the timing.

The announcer continued in her serious tone. "A young couple from Alabama are being sought as other victims of the deception. Loren and Vivian Brown are believed to have lost ten million dollars in the investment scheme. They had already left town when the news broke, but will be contacted by the Texas authorities."

"Good luck with that." Marcus crowed with laughter.

Kevin muted the sound as the rest of the table burst out laughing.

"Yeah, that's what I thought," Crawford said, before signing off.

"They can afford it." Rabi cast a narrowed look at the screen. "The Kelseys made their money working with the Russian mafia in Eastern Europe. Selling weapons that never arrived."

"They deserved it, then." Marcus cast me an unrepentant look at his summary judgement. "It's not like they stole a pension fund."

I wasn't going to lose sleep over the Kelseys' loss. Still watching the screen, I broke off in mid-laugh. "Is that them? The Browns?"

The picture on the screen, obviously taken from the hotel security camera, showed a red-headed woman with a pronounced over bite accompanied by a very stout, straggly haired man.

Kevin barely glanced at the screen before nodding. "That's them."

"No way." Marcus leaned over the table. "Are they wearing rubber masks that you peel away?"

Kevin snorted. "It's makeup and prosthetics."

"I don't see any resemblance to Safina or Fedor," I admitted. Squinting didn't help.

"Neither will the authorities." Mrs. C knotted off the end row of her creation. "That's an end, luv. Here's your wedding blanket for the both of you. A bit late but it's done."

"A present?" I eyed the large bundle of yarn that spilled onto the floor. Between the wedding and the murders, I'd paid little attention to her latest project. "I never expected one of your traditional blankets."

Kevin and Rabi both stood and reached for the blanket as Mrs. C held it out to them.

"It's a tree." Marcus yelled as the blanket was stretched out to its full width. "With a branch for each of us."

"That's amazing." The artistry and the detail were mind boggling. Each of our names was woven on a series of interconnected branches. "It's the best present I've ever received."

Marcus's branch was soft green with budding leaves. Mine and Kevin's limbs were bright green with summer's full bloom. Rabi's branch blended into autumn's gold and orange. Mrs. C's branch was bright with the blue and silver of winter.

Rabi studied it for several moments. "Beautiful."

My hubby touched the older woman's shoulder. "Thank you. This means more than you know."

Mrs. C's cheeks turned a rosy pink. "You're family, ducks."

I could have stared at it for hours, but after wiping a few tears away and exchanging hugs, I made them lay it along the back of the sofa while we cleared the table.

Settling back at the table with a mug of coffee, I put my hand over Mrs. C's and gave it a squeeze.

She responded with a soft smile.

Marcus nudged my shoulder as he sat down. "You did good yesterday."

"I'm glad it's over." Last night, I'd felt exhausted, now I was relieved. "My crossword puzzles are done. Two of them. I never expected that when we started."

"Me either." My son drummed his fists on the table. "Our biggest case, ever!"

Mrs. C's busy hands rolled up a small circle of yarn. "My money was on the pilot and his mother, the Dayton woman."

"It was a tossup until the end." I took a sip of coffee, feeling like I was coming to life. "With more time, the evidence on Jocelyn's hidden accounts would have confirmed her involvement with the fraud. Thankfully, Barsoom fingered her. Tim Dayton wasn't concerned enough to run, but Crawford said Jocelyn was headed to the airport when the police picked her up."

"Follow the money." Kevin's fingers played a rhythm on the table. "She had it."

Mrs. C stabbed the needles through the yarn. "Redmond's murder had naught to do with the others at all, did it? Completely gobsmacked me that bit."

Marcus jumped in his chair. "Barsoom did a skydiving jump the night Redmond was killed. Maybe he saw Norton load the body on the plane."

"The real irony is – no one had enough facts to expose the fraud." I tapped my phone. "Crawford texted me last night. Barsoom admitted White kept asking questions. He questioned the guy they mentioned. He discussed it with Fleming."

Rabi gave a rueful smile. "White didn't let details go."

"Fedor called it. Guilty consciences." Kevin glanced at the TV with a smile. "The fraud. Money. War medals. Olsen looking for a story. He kept digging and pushing. Jocelyn had a guilty conscience and Emerson was rattled by Olsen's knowledge of your mission. They were both on edge when they collided in the garden."

Marcus wiggled his phone as he eyed Rabi. "Olsen's story hit the web this morning. He used Kevin's headline."

"Smart man." Rabi's comment could have been meant for Kevin or Olsen, but he gave Kevin a salute with his cup.

I gave my hubby the nod as well. Takes a special touch to make a fanatic see sense.

"That's an end to our murder cases." Kevin smacked the table. He glanced at Rabi, who nodded in turn. "New order of business. The delayed honeymoon. Where do we stand?"

I gathered myself, unable to stop the grin that spread across my face. "After speaking with several people and using my own talents, which do not include the schmoozing ability of my... *our* son and my sister-in-law, the booking company president agreed to move our reservation to this weekend. He threw in tonight through Monday... at no extra cost and no penalty."

I threw up both hands and did a jig. A quick scan of the expressions revealed nothing of their inner thoughts.

I focused on Kevin. "I know it's short notice to put off jobs again. However, these are smaller jobs. I can talk to the people and buy us time."

My hubby stood up and took my hands in his. A smile teased his lips. "I've already arranged with Jimbo, Nathan, and Rabi to cover the rest of the week and Monday for B&T Handyman Inc. Mrs. C has agreed to watch Marcus again. We can leave any time."

Mrs. C resettled her ball of yarn on her lap. "We have a grand time of it, the lad and I."

The ring of faces broke out in grins.

I gasped in surprise. "When did you make the arrangements?"

Kevin shrugged. "Friday morning after you mentioned the suite was open this weekend. You were talking to your parents."

Now, I was stunned. "The guy didn't cave until this morning."

Kevin kissed my fingers. "Tracy, my love and finally my wife, I've watched you in action for ten years. I haven't bet against you since day one. I knew you'd get our balcony suite overlooking Lake Tahoe for this weekend even if we were still working on the case and couldn't go."

"I would have," I admitted. "They owed me... us."

Kevin kissed my lips. "I'll get the bags."

"Got 'em." Rabi came out of the bedroom carrying Kevin's duffle and my small suitcase still packed from Friday.

After a few hurried goodbyes and hugs, I settled in the Great White Beast next to my husband and roared down the street to my honeymoon.

Tahoe, here we come.

DEAR READERS

I'd like to welcome new readers and returning readers to the Crossword Puzzle Mystery Series. Whether you've read about the adventures of Tracy Belden and her adopted family before or you met them for the first time in this book, I hope you enjoyed their story.

It's been great fun over the last year to connect with readers who, like me, read the YA mystery series involving Trixie Belden and her group of young friends. My original inspiration for this series was to show a Trixie Belden type YA detective who'd grown up. However, Tracy had a mind of her own. Once I started writing Tracy and Marcus leapt onto the pages going full speed. Mrs. C, Rabi, and Kevin joined them and the story began.

The characters are great fun to write. I learn more about them with every book. I have to admit I don't plot out the mysteries in great detail. I'm usually as surprised as the reader when Tracy starts to unravel the clues and points to the killer.

I hope you enjoy your time in Langsdale, Nevada, and the adventures of Tracy and her adopted family. If you enjoyed the book and have the time, please leave a review at your favorite bookseller or at Goodreads.

Find me on Facebook: Louise Foster, Author

https://www.facebook.com/Louise-Foster-Author-107517717508196/?modal=admin_todo_tour

I love to hear from readers: Louise.louisefoster@gmail.com

Thank you for giving me your time to read this book and your support by buying it. I don't take either for granted.

I hope you enjoy Tracy's next case as well,

Louise Foster

MEET THE AUTHOR

I didn't pursue a writing career until I was well out of college. However, a lifelong love of reading and working on crossword and jigsaw puzzles proved to be good training when the writing bug bit. While I enjoy reading many different types of books, from thrillers to fantasy to science fiction, mysteries have always called to me.

Working on jigsaw puzzles as well as crossword puzzles with my family has also been a constant part of my life. A habit that carries through to today.

In the Crossword Puzzle Mystery Series, my love of writing and solving puzzles came together. I hope you love the quirky characters and their high-spirited adventures as much I enjoy writing them.

To learn more about the Crossword Puzzle Cozy Mystery series, visit my website www.louisefoster.com and sign up for my newsletter. An on-line crossword puzzle related to each of the books will be available on my website as each book is released.

Find me on Facebook: Louise Foster, Author

https://www.facebook.com/Louise-Foster-Author-107517717508196/?modal=admin_todo_tour

I love to hear from readers: Louise. louisefoster@gmail.com

ACKNOWLEDGMENTS

I'd like to acknowledge a few of the many people who helped make this book a reality:

My editor, Mary-Theresa Hussey, for her awesome input.

Lee Hyat, who created my beautiful book covers.

Chery Griffin, my longtime friend and critique partner. This series never would have seen the printed page without her pushing me off the cliff. Thank you.

Becky Muth, who has helped me on my post-publication path more than I can say. You rock!

ALSO BY LOUISE FOSTER

CROSSWORD PUZZLE COZY MYSTERY SERIES

An Ex in the Puzzle

Tracy Belden's first solo case in the field lands her in the middle of a murder when her ex-husband's second wife disappears and Tracy becomes a suspect.

Two Down in Tahoe

When a PI friend asks for help, Tracy and her trusty gang head to Tahoe, but things go from bad to worse when her friend goes missing and the client dies with Tracy on the scene.

Adventures in Vegas

A getaway weekend in Vegas turns dangerous when Tracy's whistleblowing client is murdered and both the secret files and a priceless golden artifact go missing.

A Question of Murder

Tracy is drawn into the world of fine art and a possible forged masterpiece when a friend's involvement in a present-day murder uncovers a hidden past and a connection to a 50-year-old murder.

Made in United States
Orlando, FL
28 June 2022

19217651R00150